W9-BLE-400

BLACKIE
AND
RED

Max Brand

is the best-known pen name of Frederick Faust, creator of Dr. Kildare, Destry, and many other fictional characters popular with readers and viewers worldwide. Born in Seattle in 1892, Faust grew up in the rural San Joaquin Valley of California. As a student at the University of California, he was considered a rebel, and was eventually denied a degree because of his unconventional conduct. Embarking on a series of adventures, he ended up in New York where he finally became a successful writer. During WWII, Faust served as a war correspondent with the infantry in Italy. He was killed during a night attack on a hilltop village held by the German army. Faust wrote prolifically for a variety of audiences, and over eighty motion pictures have been based on his work. Perhaps no other author has reached more people in more different ways.

BLACKIE AND RED

Max Brand

ROUNDUP LARGE PRINT
HAMPTON, NEW HAMPSHIRE

Library of Congress Cataloging-in-Publication Data

Brand, Max, 1892–1944.
   Blackie and Red / Max Brand.
      p.   cm.
   ISBN 0–7927–2083–0 (lg. print)
   ISBN 0–7927–2082–2 (pbk. : lg. print)
   1. Boys—Fiction.   2. Large type books.   I. Title.
[PS3511.A87B58   1994]   94–5718
813'.52—dc20   CIP

Copyright © 1924 and 1925 by Street and Smith Publications, Inc.
Renewed ® 1952 and 1953 by the Estate of Frederick Faust.
Published in Large Print by arrangement with the Golden West
Literary Agency.
All rights reserved.

Printed in Great Britain

CONTENTS

BLACKIE
AND
RED

CHAPTER ONE

JASON AND HARDWICK

The shade was thick, the wind was cool, and the burro, as usual, was tired; he reached for a long tuft of grass, found it exceedingly succulent, and fixed his grip on another tuft. Andy Connell bestowed a whack upon the rump of the little beast, but his heart was not in the blow, and the burro, being a mind-reader like most of his kind, knew that he could stay if he chose. So he leaned a little against the trunk of the nearest tree to ease the weight of the pack and continued to feed, cocking his long ears back and forth when the flies bothered him, or switching his scrubby tail half-heartedly.

Andy Connell sat down to put his back to a nearby tree and filled his pipe, and, together with the burro, he made such a picture of ease that an age-worn cow-puncher, jogging his horse past the place, drew rein and let his mustang wander into the shade, also.

'Keep that hoss away from that burro,' said Andy Connell. 'His idea of oats and hay is hoss-flesh. At workin' he's a calf, but at fightin' he's a tiger!'

The old cow hand chuckled. 'You've come a long trail to-day, I guess,' said he.

'Down from the hill, yonder,' said Connell,

1

and pointed over the roofs of the little town to a brown summit.

'Why,' said the other, 'that ain't more'n three mile.'

'Miles don't make much difference to me,' said Connell. 'Sometimes they's long, sometimes they's short.' And he tapped a rock which lay near him with a hammer which was rarely out of his hand. The rock fell asunder, and Andy Connell picked up one half and examined the fresh grain of the stone which was thus revealed.

'You been prospectin',' surmised the puncher.

'About thirty year, take it off and on,' said Connell. 'But I ain't never been too busy to take a rest.'

The cow hand pulled his long mustaches. 'Them that ride hard all day,' said he, 'and them that take it easy in the shade when they find it, I dunno but that they both get to the same place at the end of the day.'

'That's sense,' said Connell. 'That's mighty good sense. Young men don't never do no thinkin' like that. Set down here and rest yourself.'

Presently they were reclining side by side, puffing their pipes slowly, squinting through the smoke with philosophical eyes.

'What might that there house be?' asked Connell, and he pointed to the only building which was near them, a large, brown-painted house along the fence of which grew the trees whose shade they were enjoying.

'That's the orphan asylum,' said the puncher. 'Where might you be bound for?'

'Home,' said Connell without enthusiasm.

The cow hand gave him a sidelong glance. 'You're a married man,' said he gravely.

'I'm a married man,' returned Connell, and sighed.

The puncher cast up a great smoke screen. His brow was black. 'Well,' said he, 'sometimes three mile goin' home is a long day's march.'

Before Connell could answer, the door of the building opened and a stream of boys rushed out into the yard. In thirty seconds they were busy, each the member of a small group, playing, arguing, chattering, laughing. Their clamor, pitched in a scale which no mature throat could master, rang high in the air.

'It's recess, I reckon,' said the cow puncher.

'They use that for a school, too, then?'

'They do. The way the village school was run didn't please them none. So they—hello, what's that?'

A black-haired lad of ten and a red-haired boy of the same age had charged together in the midst of a swirling group which was playing a game. They paused for no preliminaries. There was only a shrill insult and a shriller retort. Then they stood toe to toe and hammered away with their fists, silently, working hard. Here were none of those round-about strokes

3

which characterize the fighting of most youngsters. They hit from the shoulder, each as straight and as true as any trained boxer. And the spatting of their fists was like the clapping of hands together.

'Red is gunna lick him!' cried Connell.

'Gimme Blackie every time,' answered the puncher. 'He's a waiter. Look at that!'

The black-haired lad, reeling back from a heavy blow, had planted himself steadily, and met the incoming rush of Red with such a tremendous thwack that the latter was tumbled head over heels.

'He's finished!' cried the cow-puncher.

'By jiminy!' said the prospector. 'Blackie don't believe in no rules!'

This he shouted as Blackie, taking note of the fall of his foe, dropped upon him and began to reach for his throat with one hand and pummel his face with the other.

'He's dropped on a tiger, though,' said the prospector. 'Look at Red fight!'

With feet and hands Red labored valiantly. Then he gripped his foeman, and they twisted over and over, head over heels, parted finally, and jumped to their feet and apart, like two battling tomcats. In the meantime, a circle of admiring spectators had gathered around them.

'Go it, Lew!' they yelled to the black-haired lad, and 'Smash him, Red!' they cried to the other.

4

They closed again, and again Blackie staggered from a pair of hard and well-placed punches.

'He ain't got the fightin' heart of Red,' said the prospector.

'He's got the fightin' brains, though,' said the puncher. 'Look at him now!' This as Blackie deftly avoided a rush and cuffed Red while the latter shot past. But Red wheeled again and lunged in for more punishment.

'Red don't know when he's hurt,' said the prospector. 'Darned if he don't fight for the love of it!'

'Brains'll beat brawn,' said his companion. 'A dollar on Blackie.'

'I'll take that. Soak him, Red!'

And Red, as though that word inspired him, landed fairly upon the point of Blackie's chin with a long and smashing punch. Blackie stumbled back, tripped over the foot of a companion, and floundered on his back.

'Looks like I've lost a dollar,' mused the cow-puncher, stroking his mustaches rapidly.

'Wait a minute,' murmured Connell.

Over the fallen combatant stood Red. 'You yaller, sneakin', scratchin' hound,' said Red, 'get up and take yer lickin'. *I* fight fair!'

Blackie writhed on the ground and rose, but as he rose, he scooped a hand around the knees of his foe and pulled him down. They collapsed together in a wriggling, fighting, kicking mass, until a teacher ran across the yard and laid hold

5

upon them. He lifted them to their feet, a pair of dusty, tattered ragamuffins.

'Jason and Hardwick,' said he through his teeth. 'This is the third time this week, and you know what I promised you. You're going to get it, and you're going to get it now. Boys, go into the house and get those two hickory switches and bring them out here. I'm going to thrash you one by one in front of the entire school. If you can be shamed into behavior worthy of young gentlemen, you *shall* be. Go at once!' He folded his arms and stood there tapping his foot on the ground, thoroughly irritated.

'Like a dog-gone woman,' said Connell. 'Darn my eyes if these here school-teachers don't make me mad. He ain't even asked who started that there fight. Well, stranger, I ain't gunna wait to see them kids licked.'

'Here's that dollar I owe you.'

'Darn that dollar. I don't want no money for what Red took out of Blackie's hide. If there'd been another two minutes, he'd of had Blackie yellin' for help. You see if he wouldn't!'

'Old son, he could fight all day and never lick Blackie. He ain't got the brains to do that! Look at 'em marchin' away for their own whips as steady as you please. I'm gunna stay and see which does the most hollerin' when they're gettin' hided!'

'Well,' muttered the prospector, as he started the burro on its way with a cruel blow, 'that sort of fun don't cost nothin'!'

6

And he was still muttering as he hurried the little animal up the road.

An hour later, two hard-riding horsemen swept up to him.

'You seen two boys—one black headed and one red—going down this way?' they asked him.

'I seen 'em fighting,' said Connell, 'but I ain't seen 'em yet.' He recognized the teacher as one of the mounted pair. 'Red was givin' him a lickin' when you come along,' he assured the latter.

'Young Hardwick,' said the teacher, 'is always the beginning of trouble. I wish to heaven that he was not in the school.'

They spurred ahead and disappeared around the next swerve of the road.

Connell followed on over the hill and down into the hollow until, in the first red of the sunset time, he saw two small, skulking forms cross the road just ahead of him and drop down beside it to drink from a spring. They waited fearlessly until Connell came up, and he found them with their shoes stripped off, cooling their feet in the water.

The record of their fight was still plainly legible on their faces, and yet even black-and-blue swellings on the cheeks and noses of a tender pink could not entirely deface them. The prospector thought them the handsomest pair of youngsters his eyes had ever seen.

Straight backed, big of neck, large of eye,

7

each with a strongly curved jaw, each with a high, deep brow, each with well-chiseled features, he could hardly say which impressed him more favorably—except that he had by nature a leaning to red hair. His own had been of that color in his youth, and there was still a rusty tint in the iron gray which covered his head.

'Where might you be bound for, young gents,' said he.

The black-haired youth gave him a mere glance and said nothing, but Red was instantly chatting.

'We're aimin' over the hill,' said he.

'Goin' home?' asked the prospector.

'Sure.'

The confidence of this lie nearly brought a betraying smile to the face of the prospector. 'You been havin' a tramp, I guess,' said he.

'We was out shootin' with air rifles,' said Red.

'Where's the rifles now?'

'Old man Clark, he seen us in his orchard. He sent his dog after us. We had to jump, you bet. The dog dog-gone near got one of us. But we dropped the guns and got over the fence in time. You could hear old Clark swearin' a mile away. That's how we got all scratched up—was gettin' away from that dog.'

This more detailed and impromptu lying pleased the prospector to the bottom of his heart. 'Well,' said he, 'it was too bad to lose

8

them guns. It ain't every day that air rifles come along your way, I guess.'

'My dad will get 'em from old Clark,' asserted Blackie, breaking into the story.

'You both in the same family?' asked the prospector.

'Him and me?' broke in Blackie, and he jerked a thumb of scorn at Red. 'Him and me in the same family?'

Red cut in swiftly and deftly. 'Sure we ain't,' said he. 'All the Hardwicks has red hair. Blackie's pa, he cooks and does odd jobs around dad's place.'

'Hey!' shouted Blackie, red with fury at this smooth insult.

'Well,' said Red calmly, 'you can't help it if your dad ain't very up in the world, can you? It ain't your fault. All the more credit to you, I guess, if you was to rise up in the world a lot and get to be—a store clerk, maybe, or something like that.'

'Why,' began Blackie, 'of all the dog-gone lyin'—'

'Wait a minute!' whispered Red, and stabbed a forefinger down the road.

Two horsemen had at that instant topped the hill. Not a word spoke either of the precious pair, but they dived for the little thicket which grew close around the spring, and there they crouched in hiding. The riders, in the meantime, drew slowly nearer, and they paused to salute the wanderer.

9

'No sign of those two young vagabonds?' asked the teacher.

'Them two you was talkin' about a while back? You ain't seen 'em?' queried the prospector.

'Not yet. But when we get them, there'll be a lesson taught them which they'll never forget, God willing!'

'What could you do to 'em?'

'Bread and water for three days or more, and confinement to the cellar for the same length of time. I'll teach them.'

'Boys is tough,' said the prospector. 'But I guess even a dog would have to learn if he got treated that way.'

'Dogs,' said the teacher, 'are tractable beasts compared with boys.'

'Well,' said Connell gruffly, 'I ain't seen either of 'em!'

So the two riders made away, and as they disappeared into the next hollow, a pair of heads popped out from the shrubbery. They reacted in different ways.

'He knew all the time,' said Blackie.

'That was mighty square of you,' said Red. 'I wouldn't of lied like that—'

'Sure you wouldn't,' said the prospector, 'not if you knowed that I knowed all the time. Now, you two look here. Where are you aimin' to go?'

'We got some trouble on our hands,' said Red. 'We want to go off somewhere and settle it.'

He turned a baleful eye upon Blackie, and Blackie glowered at him.

'What sort of trouble?' asked Connell.

'Him and me,' said Blackie, 'don't get on. One of us is the best of the two. We ain't had time for me to show him, yet, that I can lick him.'

'Who started the fighting in the first place?'

'I dunno,' said Red.

'I dunno,' said Blackie.

And they glared at one another again.

'Suppose,' said the prospector, sitting down and considering the problem, 'that you was to have it out once for all, right now. There'd be that much gained, I guess?'

'There would,' said Red, his eye shining.

'A whole pile!' said Blackie with equal joy. 'But we ain't got the time. We got to have a lot more of distance between us and the orphanage before we have it all out!'

'Well,' said the prospector, 'suppose that I was to make it safe for you?'

'Would you do that?' they cried in unison.

'I'll do that.'

'I been waitin' a long time for the chance,' shouted Blackie, and smote Red upon the crest of the nose.

'I'll tear you all apart!' shrilled Red, and hammered a hard fist into the ribs of his enemy, and in a trice they were at it.

The stand which Blackie made was a terrific

thing in so small a boy. His face deadly white, except for the streaks of crimson which stained the lower part of it—one eye swollen quite shut and the other badly puffed, he maintained a dauntless front, and still struck out with all of his might. That might could not beat off the rushes of Red, however, but it at least served to knock the latter back from time to time. Still, the end was plainly not far away. The knees of Blackie were sagging.

Between them stepped the man; against him thumped the last feeble swing of weakening Blackie. Against his breast rapped a murderous-straight punch driven in by Red.

'Hold up, you young devils!' cried the prospector.

'Lemme at him! Lemme at him!' moaned Red. 'I'm gunna get him now.'

'You little fool,' said the prospector, 'he'll knock your head off if you come in reach of him.'

'Keep back and lemme get loose at him,' gasped out the husky voice of Blackie, and he lurched forward at Red.

So doing, his foot caught on the foot of Connell, and he pitched into the dust on his face.

Connell lifted him on his arm. The lad was quite unconscious, his one open eye empty of intelligence.

'Look!' said Red, himself staggering with weakness as the battle fervor began to die

12

down in him. 'Don't you look at him, mister? He's beat. He's beat!'

'Who says he's beat?' snarled out the prospector.

'Ain't he lyin' there—near dead—all fagged?'

'I tripped him up—the fall knocked him out,' lied Connell. 'It wasn't nothing that you did to him. I stopped that fight because I seen that he was gettin' ready to soak you too hard, and I didn't want to see you hurt too bad.'

'Huh!' said Red.

It was too late to make explanations. Red had seen enough to give him assurance. The sweetness of victory took the pain from his cut face and from his well-thumped body.

Connell was already growing grave with doubts as to the wisdom of ever starting that fight when he heard Blackie groaning: 'He beat me!'

It was not the voice of a child; it was the voice of a man. And the soul of Connell grew sick in him—prophetically.

CHAPTER TWO

THE DAMAGE

What followed was, Connell felt sure, the strangest scene that was ever witnessed between two bitter rivals, between two boys, above all. Red, sick with fatigue but happy, had dropped to the ground beside the pool, and there he was washing the stains from his face and bringing himself, rapidly, back to some semblance of a human face.

He had suffered far more in features than had Blackie. The latter, fighting with more presence of mind, with more constant shrewdness, had whipped home his fists true to their aim and had cut and marked very much as he pleased.

Blackie started for the water, as his brain cleared. But he was forced to drop to his hands and knees out of sheer weakness. So he crawled to the edge of the spring, but there he dropped upon his side, fainting dead away.

Old Connell, muttering curses on the stupidity which had made him permit this contest, started to the rescue, but he stopped in amazement. For Red, leaving off the bathing of his own stinging, aching hurts, was applying himself to the relief of his enemy.

And at last, Blackie with a cleared brain said aloud: 'All right, Red. Leave me be. I dunno that I need no help from you. I guess that I can get on by myself!'

'Sure you can,' said Red. 'I thought I'd be a little help, if I could.'

At this genial attitude, Blackie was filled with suspicion. 'Are you makin' fun out of me?' he asked sharply.

14

'I ain't,' said Red.

'Because if you was, I'd start in and fight ag'in!'

'I know you would, Blackie. But I guess that I got enough for to-day.'

'I gave you a bellyful,' snarled out Blackie.

'You sure did.'

'Then keep away from me, Red. I dunno that I want your help with that water!' Blackie propped himself up on his own arms, though they were shuddering with weakness. 'I would of beat the devil out of you,' he added, 'if I'd had a good chance—if I hadn't tripped like that over his foot.'

'Maybe you would,' said Red. 'I was sure feelin' pretty sick before things ended up.'

It was most strange, most strange, but the prospector was not at all deceived. He knew that both realized that Red had won a fair victory.

'Look here, lads,' said he, 'where might you be aimin' for, the pair of you?'

'The first place that I can come to is good enough for me,' said Red calmly. 'I figger on ridin' the rods some place!'

'I dunno that I care much where I head,' said Blackie with even less enthusiasm.

'The pair of you,' said Connell, 'started out from that there asylum without no purpose in mind except to have a chance to fight things out together.'

'I guess that's it,' said Red.

15

'Well,' said Connell, 'suppose that you go back and face the music and take the lickin' that you've won. I guess it wouldn't kill you to take that?'

'I guess not,' said Red.

'I'll die first,' cried Blackie.

'That's Blackie,' said Red in a grave admiration. 'Always mighty high and proud. Dyin' ain't nothin' to him. He'd die rather'n surrender as quick as you'd snap a finger. That's the way it is with Blackie.'

Blackie lifted a high head and made no personal comment, quite contented, so it seemed, with the footnotes upon his character which Red supplied.

Then Red drew himself up a little straighter. 'I guess that I ain't gunna go back on Blackie,' said he. 'If he wants to go along, I'll go with him. But look here, Blackie,' he argued. 'There ain't much of any other place for us to go to. Back there they *got* to take care of us. That's what they're supposed to do, y'understand? But if we go along to other places, we got to work our way. I dunno that I mind workin', but I dunno that you'd take to it very kind.'

'I never done much workin',' said Blackie. 'I dunno that the Jasons ever was much for work. They always lived like gentlemen.'

'How's that you mean?' asked Red eagerly.

'Without workin' none. A gentleman, he's a guy that don't so much as lift his hand.'

Here there was a chuckle.

16

'Ain't that right?' asked Red of the prospector.

'I guess it's right a lot of the time,' said Connell.

'Well,' said Blackie, 'all of my folks was gentlemen. They never done no work. Before the war, they used to have piles of slaves. After the war they still was rich. But sneaks come and took their money. That was in the old days. My pa had to work some. But he didn't do no more'n he had to. He just kep' along until he up and died, one day. That was all I know about it, except that it won't do for a Jason to work.'

'How'll you get along, then?' asked Red curiously.

'I guess they's ways,' said Blackie Jason with marvelous calm. 'I guess that I ain't the first gentleman in the world that's growed up without workin' for his keep.'

'I s'pose not,' said Red very seriously. 'It's all got to begin somewheres, or else we wouldn't have no gentlemen in the world, would we?'

'I guess that we wouldn't,' said Blackie in agreement with himself. 'You got sense, Red. You can see things. You'd ought to see why I can't go back to that there place.'

'I dunno that I do, though, Blackie.'

'Well, we'd get licked, wouldn't we, as soon as we come back?'

'I guess you ain't scared of a lickin',' said Red with much faith. 'I guess that wouldn't keep you away none.'

'I been licked twice before,' said Blackie darkly.

'I know it. And I seen you stand up and take it without never so much as winkin' an eye. That's why I know that it wouldn't keep you away none.'

'You're wrong, Red. The first time that I was licked, that was for throwin' an eraser at that cross-eyed little skunk—Jimmy Dover.'

'I disremember the day. But I recollect the lickin' in front of the whole schoolroom. You'd of thought that the teacher was givin' you ice cream and pie—you didn't stir! It was pretty fine. That day was what showed us all that you was different from the rest of us. Take me, for instance, Blackie. Dog-gone me if I ain't swore that when I was up to take a lickin' I wouldn't make a sound. But the minute I began to get it I got so mad and so scared and besides it *stung* so dog-gone bad that I just couldn't help bellerin', no matter how much I hated myself afterward.'

After this relation, there was a pause.

'I guess that you and me are a mite different,' said Blackie at last.

'I guess that maybe we are.'

'What did you feel like doin' afterward?'

'For about five minutes I sure wanted to kill the teacher. Afterward I sort of forgot about it.'

'Well,' said Blackie slowly, 'I don't never forget, and all that I want to do every minute is to get at that there teacher. After the last time

18

that he caned me, I swore that I'd cut his throat if he ever licked me ag'in. That's why I don't want to go back. A gentleman like a Jason, he sure has to keep his oaths, don't he? And I don't want to go back to that school, because there'll be a murder in the makin' mighty quick if I do!'

So said Blackie, and Red, in an awe-stricken silence, agreed that this reasoning was very high and very good.

'All right,' broke in Connell, who had listened with smiles to this entire dialogue of childish reason. 'If you ain't gunna go back to the school, how would you like to tramp about seventy-five mile with me and take up with me in my house?'

'Why, jiminy Christmas,' said Red. 'We ain't got no right over you, mister!'

'Shut up,' said Blackie rather sharply. 'Maybe the gentleman would have some sort of use for us around his place!'

There was such respect in his voice, and there was such a reverent accent upon the 'gentleman,' that Connell was flattered in spite of himself.

'Sure,' said Red. 'I can work like the dickens! I can do anything from broncho bustin' to milkin' cows. That's how handy I am.'

'Ain't you got no kids of your own?' asked Blackie cautiously.

'Not a one.'

'Nor no wife, even?' asked Blackie.

19

The prospector stopped short as he was pacing up and down, his heart warmed by the thought of the good action which he had in contemplation.

'My Lord,' he breathed. 'I forgot clean all about her!'

CHAPTER THREE

HOMEWARD BOUND

It was a bitter fight which Mr Connell waged with his soul as he stood there in the road under the pallor of the growing stars and made his heart big to face the thought of what his wife would say if he brought home two pairs of unproductive hands.

Beside him, Red was chattering busily, telling how many things he could do, and what he could make with hammer and saw and nails, until Blackie stopped him short.

'Don't go botherin' him,' said Blackie. 'I guess he don't need your advice none!'

So Red was quiet, and at last, the prospector summoned the full height of his resolution and made his heart strong.

'Boys,' said he, 'we're goin' home!'

They camped that night in the hollow on the other side of the hill, and there Blackie, in spite of the disdain which he had expressed for work, proved himself the more useful of the pair. Red, in fact, was bothered by a pair of eyes, one of which was swollen quite shut and the other of which was so battered and bruised that he could look out upon the world through a narrow slit, only.

In this condition, he merely stumbled here and there, doing his best, but making a poor job of that. But Blackie, though still a little shaky on his legs, was very cheerful, and quite efficient, and above all, he was very respectful.

They found out all about Andy Connell's name, and his occupation, or rather lack of any occupation.

'I'd aim to say that the Connell family was a pretty old one,' said Blackie.

'I dunno,' said Connell. 'But it appears to me that I've heard it said that the Connells goes back pretty far.'

'I could tell,' declared Blackie. 'It ain't easy to fool me about that. I got a sort of an instinct for tellin' a gentleman when I see him. It ain't the way he talks; it ain't the way he's dressed; but it's just sort of something on the inside of him.'

'I might be askin' you, Red,' said Connell, 'what's your real name?'

'Oliver Hardwick is what I'm called.'

'That's a pretty smart-sounding name. Who was your folks?'

'I seen my father once. My ma died before I could remember nothin'. My father was a fine-

21

talkin' old gent. He had a scar between his eyes that made him look mighty fierce. But that's about all that I remember of him. Why might you be askin'?'

'I didn't know,' said Connell, 'but what you might be out of a family as good as Blackie, yonder.'

'Me? Oh, no! Blackie, he's out of quality folks. You could see that in a minute, I guess. Couldn't you?'

Mr Connell regarded him with thought for some time. Then: 'We all got to take our chances with things,' said he. 'We all got to take our chances, and I'm willin' to take a chance with Blackie. *You* like him, Red?'

'Me? Sure, I do. But you see, Blackie is worth about ten common boys like me!'

'H-m-m,' said Connell, and said no more.

It was the third day after this—for Connell did not believe in long, forced marches, as has been said, when at last they came, in the evening of the day, within sight of a log hut built upon the side of a rocky hill which sloped into forty acres of level meadow land, a skirting of brush and of trees around the field.

'There,' said Connell, 'is my house, and there's the place which I hope that the pair of you'll be able to call home. God and the missus willin'!'

He added: 'Wait over here by these here trees. I'm gunna go ahead and see how things is.'

22

He departed.

'He ain't the chief guy in his own house,' said Blackie. 'His wife is the one. Mrs Connell is the one that we got to learn how to handle.'

'Her?' said Red vaguely. 'Well, I dunno. Mr Connell is my boss!'

'He ain't nobody's boss,' said Blackie. 'He can't even run himself!'

The prospector, in the meantime, reached the door of his cabin. It was the rear door to which, after a slight hesitation, he directed his steps. And when he stood in it, with the well-worn boards of the kitchen floor before him, he found Mrs Connell in the act of drawing newly baked bread from the oven. His heart leaped. Certainly there could not have been a more propitious moment. He regarded the bread with an anxious eye. Yes, it was all good, golden brown, and therefore her heart must be warmed with self-satisfaction.

'Well, Frederica,' said he, 'here I be, home ag'in.'

He always used her full name when he desired to be most ingratiating. Otherwise, he called her Rica, an abbreviation which she detested.

She still kept half an eye on the bread as she whirled upon him. 'Here you are back,' said she, 'but how much good luck did you bring back with you, Andy Connell?'

'I struck a fine lead,' said Andy, sitting down by the stove, but keeping a wary watch upon

23

his better half.

'But it petered out,' suggested his wife.

He coughed. 'A gent can't *always* have bad luck,' said he. 'Some time it's got to turn.'

'Not so long's he plays the fool!' said Mrs Connell fiercely. 'If you got *any* sense, Mr Connell, you'll stop thinkin' of this here idiotic prospectin' after gold, and you'll start ploughin' and sowin' your own good land.'

'Good land,' groaned he. 'It ain't worth nothin' except to raise rocks.'

'Bah,' said she. 'You never gave it a chance. Dodgin' work, say I!'

He held forth his calloused hands. 'Did I get these playin'?' he asked sadly.

She had begun in a note of indignant protest, she had run on to passionate denunciation, and from this she declined upon tearful self-pity. Mr Andrew Connell had listened to the first part of this speech with growing dread, but when at last he saw her drop into a chair and lift her apron to her face, he drew a great breath of relief and hastening to the door, he waved his hand. Instantly the two boys were over the fence and standing before him.

'She's took to tears,' said he. 'When she comes to and sees you and knows why you're here, she'll start whoopin' it up ag'in. And then they ain't nothin' for you to do except to say nothin' and stand still, but don't answer back. You hear?'

And they nodded gravely. Their sympathy

24

was for him as much as for themselves, for they had to endure the pest only for the moment, so to speak, whereas with him it was a recurring calamity, sweeping away the sweetness of life every year in a devastating harvest.

Mr Connell brought the boys into the house and spoke gently to his wife. 'Here you are, Frederica. Dog-gone me if our bad times ain't about over. Yes, sir. Here we got enough hands, and willing hands, to make the work of farmin' this place mighty light, say I!'

The weeper lifted her head and saw before her the pair of boys. Immense anguish inspired her. The full truth burst upon her prophetic brain.

'You brung 'em both home to live with *us!*'

'Yes, sir,' grinned her husband. 'Ain't that fine, Rica?'

Mrs Connell glared at him, but words were too weak. Her gaze passed through him and above him. She raised her hands to the deity which presides over tormented wives.

'Oh, Lord,' moaned Mrs Connell, 'why was I married to a fool? What have I done to deserve a husband like him?'

Then wild passion leaped into her brain. Automatically she reached behind her, but before she could complete the gesture, Mr Connell had seized a boy under each arm and scooped them across the threshold and around the corner of the cabin. There, pausing and peering cautiously back, they saw the flatiron

25

shoot through the open doorway. It thudded against the trunk of a sapling, gouging out a great chunk of soft bark and showing the white rind of the young tree.

'How come you to stand for it?' asked Blackie sharply. 'Don't she belong to you?'

The prospector blinked down at the youth. 'You mean, by the law, son?' he murmured. 'Sure, by the law she may be. But don't think that law means nothin' to women. They make up their own law, and it's a dog-gone sight stronger than any law that men can get together. Come along with me!'

He took them back among a little group of orchard trees. There he sat down and motioned to them to do likewise.

'Look here,' said Red, anxiously, 'ain't it right that we should start out and try to find a campin' place if we ain't gunna put up here?'

'Always aimin' at some more walkin'!' sneered Blackie. 'I never see such a boy! Look here, Red, d'you aim to know more'n a growed up man like Mr Connell, maybe?'

'Well,' said Red, 'I think maybe that I'd try to find a way of handlin' 'em. I'd hate to say that I was licked by nothin' but a girl!'

'But how could you fight 'em?' asked Blackie. 'A gent couldn't be fightin' a girl, could he?'

'Settin' still and waitin' for time to take care of itself, that's a mighty sight the best way to get on with the girlfolks and the womenfolks,'

26

stated Mr Connell. 'You watch, now, and see!'

He leaned back in a comfortable hollow and lighted his pipe.

'Well, sir,' said he, 'God had the intention of givin' the womenfolks a mighty easy time in the world, while the men are a-slavin' and a-toilin' to keep 'em comfortable and to keep 'em idle!'

'Seems to me,' put in Red, 'that I ain't seen many womenfolks that was havin' a particular easy time.'

'You ain't?' asked the prospector dryly. 'You've seen 'em workin' pretty hard, maybe?'

'Fair to middlin',' declared the boy earnestly.

'A gent like you,' said the prospector, 'will grow up to be about seventy. Your granddaughters will be workin' you and a-slavin' you before you wake up and see what you're headed for. Yes, sir, that's about the way it'll be with you!'

Here a bell clattered from the house. And Mr Connell exclaimed softly with great satisfaction.

'That there,' said Blackie, 'sounds like the dinner bell was a-ringin'. What could it mean except that she's a-callin' us?'

'It couldn't mean nothin' but that,' declared the prospector, 'but it ain't our time to move yet. Don't never do nothin' fast with womenfolks, son. Always give 'em time. Give 'em lots of time. They'll hang themselves if they got rope enough. But keep 'em short and they'll hang *you*!'

Thus monologued Mr Connell as he worked at his pipe. Eventually the door of the cabin was knocked open and the tall and robust form of Mrs Connell appeared.

'Hey, Mr Connell!' called she. 'Hey, Connell!'

'Git up,' whispered Mr Connell covertly. 'Git up and start that burro down the hill, will you? Git up, and come along with me. Keep your back turned to the house, and walk along steady and slow, but don't never look back nor pay no attention to her. That'll bring her to time, by crackie! That'll make her come to time!'

So the three, and the burro along with them, started down the hill through the orchard. And, at once, the eye of Mrs Connell caught upon the moving forms.

'Andy!' yelled his better half. 'D'you hear me? Are you gone deaf?'

Now she was running after them.

'Listen!' whispered Mr Connell. 'Durn me if she ain't comin' running. Brains is what them needs that would work with women. Yes, sir, brains is what they got to have. Listen to her comin' runnin' after me. Now, would a man of believed his ears or his eyes that heard or seen her a little while back drivin' us out into the evenin'?'

Mrs Connell came storming upon them. 'Is this the way you're sneakin' off, Andy

28

Connell?' cried she.

Mr Connell took his pipe from his mouth. He dropped his other hand upon his hip. It was a grand gesture!

'Ma'am,' said he, 'I guess we've listened to the worst you could say about us. But if you got more insults to pass about us, we'll stay right here and listen some more. We aim to act like gentlemen, ma'am.'

'Don't stand there ma'amin' me like a great big booby,' said Mrs Connell more gently, 'but get back into that house and eat your supper. I can see your hungry eyes, you rascals.'

Then she lurched after him and caught him by the arm: 'Andy, do you mean it? Are you leavin' me for good?' she whispered, in such a voice that it sent a chill down the body of Red.

'I ain't makin' no threats,' said Andy Connell. 'I'm sayin' good-by, ma'am. I've stood enough, I guess, and this here to-night is about the finish.'

'Oh,' cried Mrs Connell, 'why was I ever born!'

And, bursting into violent and noisy weeping, she fell into the arms of her spouse. The latter received her on his broad breast and at the same time winked through the dusk at his two confederates and with a motion of his head signaled to them to go on to the cabin.

CHAPTER FOUR

A BROKEN PLOW

To Red it seemed a most unusual home-coming. But in five minutes Mrs Connell had quite recovered from all her emotion. Her eye was clear as a summer sky which a recent shower has washed. Her step was light and brisk, and her voice was continually trailing away in the humming of some fragment of song. Except for the 'Old Brown Jug,' she did not know her way through any song from beginning to end.

In the meantime, she heaped upon the table enough food to have fed thirty, instead of three. And the two boys and Connell, literally letting out their belts, fell to on the good provisions with a wonderful will. Plate after plate was emptied, and still they struggled forward valiantly until, at last, they could perform no more.

Then they pushed back their chairs, Red to close his eyes and drowse with fatigue and delicious sleepiness, and Connell to pull forth his black and polished pipe, which he presently filled and lighted. But Blackie, forcing himself up with a great effort of the will, started to clear the table of its dishes.

Mrs Connell was immensely impressed.

30

First she snatched the dishes from his hands.

'This home of mine,' she declared, 'ain't one where a boy is turned into a girl, havin' to do kitchen work. No, young man. You do a boy's part around here and I'll try to do a woman's work. You been bad beat, poor child! I'll have to lay some raw meat to that face of yours to-night.'

'Ma'am,' said Blackie, 'I dunno that I can find the right words to thank you for takin' us in to-night.'

'The others ain't bothering about thanks,' said Mrs Connell. 'Women that have to do with men, they don't expect no thanks. Heaven knows that we was made slaves from the beginning. All work and no pay and that's our lives.'

This she said with a great sigh, but with one thick forearm laid upon his shoulders and with one red hand patting his arm.

'You're a good boy,' said Mrs Connell. 'Redhead, yonder, I guess he don't care none what's done for him.'

'He ain't had much bringin' up, I guess,' said Blackie.

All of this, in the meantime, Red heard. His eyes had been half closed with delicious weariness, but he had wakened to hear this bit of dialogue, and now he was ashamed to open them and look up again.

But afterward, when he and Blackie slept side by side in the attic room, Red dreamed of

31

vengeance for the sly and underhanded thrust which his companion had dealt him in the good esteem of Mrs Connell.

When the next day came, he decided that he had been thrust down so low in her esteem that it would be useless for him to make any attempt to regain her good opinion. He had only one hope, and that was to succeed doubly with Mr Connell. Or, perhaps best of all, roll his blanket and start on the long out-trail.

When breakfast was served, it was plain that Mrs Connell had formed her first prejudices strongly in favor of Blackie. She called him by the full name of 'Lewis' and reproved her husband for calling him 'Lew.' 'There ain't no dignity,' said she, 'about a name like that. And Lewis is a dignified boy. Look how straight he stands! If I had a son, now, I'd be havin' one like Lewis. No blatherin' about that boy!'

But Red was not a favorite with her. She disapproved of the manner in which his hair thrust up behind, defying comb and brush and even liberal dousings of water. She objected to his freckles, also.

'Them freckles look like rust to me,' she said. 'They make me want to get some soap and a scrubbin' brush after 'em.'

And before breakfast was half over, she was at her husband with her plans. He was to begin the plowing at once. She had been working out in the village and had managed to save up a little money which she would invest in seed.

And if the grain were sowed now, it would not be too late for the autumn harvesting.

In the end, Mr Connell put in for himself, but not until the meal was finished, because, as he said to Red afterward, it is always best to be sure of one's provisions before starting an argument with one's wife. One should be ready, always, to start on a long march well provided. What he had to say now was that he could not do the plowing until he had sharpened the plow shares.

'All right,' said Mrs Connell. 'I might of knowed that nothin' would start the way I wanted it. But you start in sharpenin' the shares. I'll have the seed up here to-morrow. If you do some plowin' this afternoon, I can start in with the sowing the next day after.'

All of this was not so easily accomplished, because in the first place the little blacksmith shop which was attached to the barn needed repairing before the forge could be worked. The bellows had a great hole torn in them, and the careful patching of the hole occupied the first day throughout, with Red helping as best he could.

Blackie was detached by Mrs Connell and sent on various errands as far as the village, to which he rode, sending his whistle before him; or else he was retained to chatter with her as she worked in the house.

'Good looks is what the womenfolks like,' said the prospector sagely to Red. 'But a strong hand is what menfolks want.'

The second day saw the repairing of the forge itself, for the draft was choked even after the bellows had been repaired. The third day was Sunday, and the speech of Mr Connell when his wife urged him to work on the Sabbath was a pathetic masterpiece, which rang in the ears of Red for days thereafter.

'Because,' said Mr Connell, 'there ain't no way that a man can get ahead of God, and when God says for a man to rest, he'd better obey.'

'Then,' said Mrs Connell with a grim emphasis, 'God must be speakin' with you all the time, Andy.'

The fourth day of the work at length witnessed the sharpening of the shares. There were two of them in the little gang plow which was to rip up the rich soil of the meadow land, and after the rusted bolts had been turned and the shares taken off, and after they had been screwed securely into place again when the sharpening was ended—with Red using the tongs and working the bellows—the fourth day had ended.

On the fifth day the team was assembled. It consisted of an old gray mule which had once been black, but which time and gathering wisdom had given a new coat. There was a span of ancient geldings which had been carriage horses on a time, then cow ponies, and finally they were too slow for anything but the plow, and too weak for that. The fourth horse in the team was a young two-year old, all length of leg and neck, and full of coltish fire and folly. The first thing he did was to plunge through the rotten harness which held him to the plow, and so the fifth day was spent repairing, with odds and ends and baling wire, the damage which he had done.

The next morning out came Mrs Connell to watch the work begin.

'You've took six days to harness up a plow team, Andy,' she said. 'Heaven only knows how long it'll take you to plow an acre of ground!'

Mr Connell sighed and shook his head. 'I been busy every minute,' said he. 'You can ask Red if I've wasted a single second, except for the fillin' of my pipe.'

'Bah,' cried Mrs Connell. 'Two liars, the pair of you.'

And she stamped away toward the cabin. At length the team was harnessed, however, and the plow was rolled down to the meadow land. The lever was raised which allowed the shares to descend upon the ground, the word was spoken, and the whip snapped which sent the horses into the collars, and after skidding along the grassy surface for a moment, the shares began to bite. With a sound like the tearing of cloth, they cut through the grass roots, then, sliding deeper, they began to sink in the soft earth while the team, finding several tons of burden on them, slackened at once to that patient, hopeless, deep-nodding walk of the typical plow team. But slow though they went, the plow was busy.

Mr Connell enjoyed the work hugely. He showed Red how to handle the reins. Then he followed along, walking on the ground where the surface was firm and letting Red stumble among the clods. But while Red labored, Mr Connell sang, and his voice was gay as the voice of a lark.

Then, just before noon, came tragedy to darken the day. The plow had been dragged to the hillward top of the meadow and then turned down the slope. With the pull of gravity to lighten the load behind him, and with the itch of a sore shoulder to madden him, the colt leaped forward with a snort. It was only the work of a moment.

'Hold tight onto them reins!' cried Connell.

But Red might as well have attached himself to the flying tail of a comet. He dangled vainly at the end of the reins while that entire rickety team caught a foolish alarm and plunged into a ridiculous gallop. For thirty yards they gathered speed, with the plow skipping lightly above the surface of the grass. Then there was a crash. The team stopped. Red pulled himself to his feet, still clutching the reins, and there, before him, was a broken plow. The steel standard which braced the shares had snapped squarely in two, and just in front of the plow

36

shares, scarred by the dint of their points, was the jutting rock which had caused the damage.

Mr Connell came slowly forward. For a moment he looked black upon Red, but then he shrugged his shoulders. Since his Sabbath talk he had become a religious man, at moments.

'I ain't gunna be able to face Rica,' said he. 'But still, it don't look like God wanted this here field to be plowed. What does it look like to you, Red? Unhitch the hosses and take them back to the barn!'

The horses were unhitched; and Red, coming back from backing them to the barn, found Mr Connell had moved the broken plow and that he was addressing the stone which had caused the wreck.

'Rocks was made to be the things that was to beat me,' said Connell. 'Yes, sir, rocks is the things that I've follered all of my life. They's the ruin of me. Dog-gone my soul if they ain't!' And he kicked the rock with his heel, gently.

Behold! the stout rock fell apart at that touch. The plow shares had cracked it, and now a reddish, shining interior, singularly patterned with veins, was revealed.

The pipe dropped from between the teeth of Mr Connell and struck on the toe of his boot.

'Well, darn me!' whispered he.

'What's the matter?' asked Red, amazed.

'Nothin', boy, nothin'!' cried the prospector roughly. 'You got them hosses unharnessed?'

37

'You didn't say for me to,' objected Red.

'I'm sayin' it now. You run along and get that team unharnessed and turn 'em out into the corral and then clean out the side of the barn they was in and then throw down some feed to 'em.'

'Are you mad with me?' asked Red.

'Gone and broke the best plow I ever owned,' thundered Connell. 'Ain't that enough to make me mad, young feller?'

Full of the black injustice of this remark, Red wandered back to the barn and began his task.

It was a long hour before he finished, and as he came back through the corral, he saw Mr Connell climbing hastily along the edge of the rocky brow which overlooked the same meadow where the plow had just been broken. Now and again he paused and stooped, as though he found interesting stories in the stones he walked upon. After that, he went on again, and dropped out of sight beyond the ridge.

CHAPTER FIVE

CONNELL DISAPPEARS

'And we ain't gunna see him no more,' said Mrs Connell, when that day grew dark. 'We ain't gunna have Mr Connell back with us no more. When he seen that there wasn't no place for him in this here house unless he was willin' to do his work every day, he sort of lost interest in everything. I guess that I seen it comin' as clear as anybody.'

So said Mrs Frederica Connell, standing in her door with her arms akimbo, shaking her head at the advancing night.

'Oliver Hardwick,' said she, without turning her head. 'Maybe *you're* too proud to work?' she went on, as Red jumped up and went toward her.

'I'm reasonable willin' to work,' said Red, 'but I ain't gunna stay on here and be no bother to you, Mrs Connell.'

'Go bring in some wood,' said Mrs Connell, 'and don't be answerin' back.'

Red endured this insult in silence. After all, the autumn was ending. The cold of the winter was not far away, and to be cast out upon the world in that bitter season would be sad indeed. So, quietly, he made up his mind that he would spend the entire winter in the cabin and take whatever ill treatment came his way from Mrs Connell, or from her favorite, Blackie.

When the winter ended, he could shift for himself in the spring. In warm weather, he had no fear of traveling, but in the chill of the winter travel was another matter, as he very well knew.

39

These conclusions he reached while he was getting the armful of wood. When he came back through the kitchen door, the voices of Mrs Connell and of Blackie, which had been busy before his arrival, grew suddenly and suspiciously silent. Blackie had the corner seat, between the fire and the window, and there he was curled up in the greatest comfort, reading a book, or pretending to read it. But there was a twitching at the corners of his mouth by which Red knew that there was trouble ahead in the air.

Mrs Connell said savagely, as she crashed some pans together in the dish water: 'Young man, I guess that laziness is a ketchin' bug. I guess that laziness sure does take up on folks. Maybe you was a mighty active, busy boy till you come here, but the same dog-gone thing that's in Andy Connell has took hold on you, now. How long will it be takin' you to walk a mile if it takes you this long to bring in some wood?'

To this, Red discreetly answered nothing. But he retired to a corner and sat down to brood over this injustice. He had hardly settled himself when the voice of Mrs Connell snapped shrewishly after him: 'Look what you trailed in here. Look at all this dust. You jump right up, young man, and get a broom and sweep this out!'

This was adding insult to injury, but Red gloomily rose and found the broom and began

40

to sweep. He was through with this task when, turning suddenly from it, he surprised a smile of intelligence and wicked pleasure passing between the woman and Blackie. It was clear that Blackie himself had a hand in the contriving of all of this mischief. How did the great spirit of Red swell in his heart. But he endured, and he said nothing. After all, these were mere petty goadings of his spirit, and he could stand them all winter long, if need be.

The next morning the frost was on the ground, and when Red came down the stairs, he was given the bucket and told to go out and milk the cows. It was a mighty task. The old, red cow was an easy affair, but the roan was a demon with sharp horns and ready heels. When at last Red, having cornered her in the corral, had added two gallons of milk to the one which he drew from the red, and when he was about to carry in the treasure, the roan flicked her heel forward and spilled two thirds of the contents. He rose and looked down at the bucket in dismay. For he knew very well that this accident would be made a means of goading him.

He was right. When he entered the house with his explanation, Blackie, from beside the stove, where he sat yawning and shivering, and warming himself, snickered behind his hand, at the sight of the bucket, and hearing Red's words.

'You stumbled and spilled it, you mean,'

shrilled Mrs Connell. 'No, you didn't milk old roan at all. That ain't more'n the red cow's milk. Young feller, has my old man taught you to lie like this, or have you took to it nacheral?'

Once more Red swallowed the insult.

For a week it was like this. All the outside work was given to his share. All the wood chopping with a frosted ax, all the milking twice a day, all the feeding of the pigs with swill, and the repairing of the roofs when the shakes dropped off the barn, and the rebuilding of the fence when the stray steers broke through; all of these items were added to his moiety of the work.

As for Blackie, Mrs Connell was constantly praising him for his industry and for his efficient workmanship, but all that he did was to help with the washing of the dishes, wash a window now and then, build or renew a fire, or scrub down the front veranda which was built across the face of the little cabin. His work was really no work at all, and poor Red knew it very well. And at the table, the best bits of meat, the largest piece of pie, all fell to the share of Blackie, and he absorbed all of these favors with a smug air, and with many taunting glances, which maddened Red.

After a meal ended, Blackie and Mrs Connell would sit for a long time chatting confidentially together. Mrs Connell at times was moved to narrate a story, sometimes sad and sometimes gay, and whatever she said, the applause of Blackie was assured for her. His murmuring admiration and his loud laughter sometimes so grated upon the ears of Red that he felt he could endure it no more, but when these times came, there was nothing left for him to do except to leave the house and shut the hateful sounds from his ears.

He decided upon one thing. Before he left, in the spring, he would corner Blackie and beat him almost to death. Then he would drag the limp body to the lady of the house, show her what he had done to her favorite and disappear.

This prospect became a haunting thing. He could not forget it. He dreamed of it at night, and at last he decided that he could not wait until the spring came.

One night they clambered up to bed in the attic.

'You look kind of fagged, Red,' said Blackie.

'A mite,' said Red, 'but I ain't too tired to about murder you, Blackie, one of these days. So, keep care of yourself.'

'Oh,' said Blackie, 'I'll keep care of myself, right enough.' And he laughed in a way which Red could not understand.

'Besides,' said Blackie, 'there never was a time that you could beat me, if they was somebody standin' around to make you fight fair.'

To this taunt, Red answered not a word. He

wanted to be fresh for this great work. So he waited until the harsh voice of Mrs Connell roused him in the morning. Then he stood up and dressed and hurried outdoors. In the barn he pitched a few forkfuls of hay, just enough to warm his blood and his body and loosen his muscles. Then he hurried back to the house and into the attic, where Blackie was still yawning and stretching in the bed.

'Git up, Blackie,' he whispered. 'The old brown dog has got a litter out in the shed.'

What boy could resist such news as this? Blackie, at least, could not. For a moment he suspiciously scanned the face of his companion, but then the gleaming eyes and the suffused face of the latter seemed to convince him.

'Wait a minute,' he said. 'I'm gunna go back with you.'

He wakened fully, stretched for the last time, and dived into his clothes, while Red stood by, wondering. Never could he dress with such lightning celerity as Blackie showed, and even his most careful work could hardly match the fastest of Blackie's for neatness when all was done! Indeed, he felt often in the presence of Blackie, a superior intellect, a superior bodily equipment. It was no wonder that Mrs Connell preferred the boy to him; not her judgment but her unfairness maddened Red, for there is no enthusiast so keen for good sportsmanship as your typical American boy.

The chill of the morning air, when they started out, meant nothing to the racing blood of Red, but it made Blackie stop and shudder. Then he hurried on, beating his body with his hands to increase the speed of the circulation.

'What sort of color was they?' he asked breathlessly as they turned the corner of the shed.

'They was all red,' said Oliver Hardwick, and as he spoke, since the shed was between them and the house and screened them from view of Mrs Connell, he whirled and smote the cheek of Blackie with the full flat of his hand, a stinging blow. Blackie reeled back against the wall of the shed.

'You—skunk!' he gasped out. 'Mrs Connell'll turn you out of doors for this.'

'She ain't gunna have no time for turnin',' snarled out Red. 'I'm gunna leave. Her and you can spend the winter- and you can do all of the outside chores. But I'm gunna eat you up small, Blackie, before I'm through. You stand up and fight!'

'Fight?' said Blackie, attempting to bluster his way through this bad predicament. 'Why, kid, when I get through with you, there ain't gunna be enough left for the buzzards to fly after! Git out of my way, Red, or I'll bust your head open!'

So saying, he doubled his fists and swelled his chest. Red could not answer. The fierce certainty of triumph, the deadly joy of the

45

combat to come, made him mute. He could only grin in a ghastly fashion upon Blackie. Then he smote him suddenly and heavily upon the chin—a long, whipping, straight punch which he had practiced among the shadows of the barn, many times before.

The results of it were amazing. Blackie, to be sure, was no longer the stalwart of a month before. Soft living had undermined his strength for striking as well as his strength for resisting. At least, this blow, landing flush upon the end of his chin, bowled him backward off his feet, crashed his shoulders against the wall of the shed, and then dropped him with the recoil upon his face in the mud.

To Red, looking down on his victim, this was a tragedy too bitter to be contemplated. Better, far better, to take many a ringing blow from the foe so long as he might, himself, have the exquisite privilege of painting the features of Blackie the thickest and most dripping crimson. But to have a battle ended by a single blow.

He stood back, half scornful, half sad. And he saw Blackie pick himself slowly from the mud and stand up—black indeed after that groveling moment on the earth.

'I'll stand up to you!' he gasped out at Red. 'Darn you if I don't put you down as dog-gone low as I was!' And, so saying, he swung the stick with a will in both hands. It clipped Red only a glancing blow. Even that graze was enough to topple him to his knees. He lurched up and strove to duck under the second blow and get at his enemy with his hand. But red lightning out of a black cloud struck him. The red light flared across his vision, and then he dropped into utter unconsciousness.

CHAPTER SIX

A TIMELY ARRIVAL

Here he lay for some time. And at length, when he opened his eyes, he was not lying in the mud, but in the warmth of the kitchen.

The voice of Blackie was explaining in the distance: 'I know you seen me, Mrs Connell. You seen me hit him with the stick, but you dunno the reason why. It was him that got me out there, sayin' that he had some puppies to show me in the shed. When he got me there, he told me that he was tired of workin' here for you and that what he wanted to do first of all was to try to kill me. Then he grabbed up that stick and hit me—you see that bruised place on my chin?'

'The little demon!' cried Mrs Connell. 'Poor Lewis!'

'He knocked me right down into the mud. You see how my clothes are fixed?'

'He'd ought to be skinned alive!'

'But I got up and dove into him and got the stick away!'

'Lewis, you're a brave boy.'

'And then I hit him!'

What could Red do? He thought it over, blinking and winking. But his mind could not function clearly. There was a blinding pain which passed from the front of his head to the back. He raised his hand and found a great lump had been raised along the right side of his skull. Then he struggled into a sitting posture. Mrs Connell and Blackie stood above him.

'You young imp of Satan!' said the severe Mrs Connell. 'You get up and get out. There ain't gunna be no need for you around this house no more. A murderin', sneakin', stupid youngster like you'll grow into a murderin', sneakin', idle man. Oliver Hardwick, I don't want to see no more of your face ag'in. *Git!*'

He stood up, reeling, sick, and before he could answer, he was aware of a newcomer—none other than Andy Connell himself, who stood in the doorway with a stick in one hand and a knife in the other, paring off long, thin shavings with scrupulous care and from time to time glancing up to follow the movements and the talk and the expressions on the other faces.

'Mr Connell,' cried Red. 'I'm mighty glad to see you. I was hatin' to leave before I had a chance to say good-by to you.'

'Well,' said Connell, 'I'm sorry that you're tired of stayin' on here with me, and Mrs

48

Connell.'

Mrs Connell, in the meanwhile, had turned sharply around and beheld her spouse. Her astonishment, at first, made her pale. But rage followed after and made her equally red again. Then, by a mighty effort of the will, she controlled her voice.

'You've come back, maybe,' said she, 'to do the plowin' and finish up the work?'

'Might be,' said her husband, looking into her face with a singular intentness, 'that I have.'

'Then go back where you come from!' screamed Mrs Connell. 'You know mighty well that the time for the plowin' is past and done for. God knows how we're gunna pass over the winter. And I ain't gunna have the weight of *you* on my hands! I don't need you. I don't want you. You ain't welcome here. Go back to your other tramps and loafin' bums, Mr Andrew Connell. I hope that I never have to set eyes on your face ag'in! Never, as long as I live.'

And with this, she laid hands upon the nearest weapon—it was only a broom, but a broom in the hands of Mrs Connell was a formidable tool. She did not use it as a club, in which capacity it was quite harmless, but as a lance. She had dug more than one handle into the ribs of her spouse before this day.

But, to her bewilderment, and to the surprise of the two boys, who looked on, half grinning with expectancy, Andy Connell turned slowly away.

There was no sudden dive for the doorway and the freedom of the great outdoors. Instead, he crossed the room, and took off his overcoat, and hung it upon the nearest nail. Then he turned back to the stove and stood there, warming his hands.

'The man's gone daft!' breathed Mrs Connell. 'Mind your muddy feet.'

Then, staring again at the boots of Mr Connell, she saw for the first time that there was no mud on them! Indeed, a second and more scrupulous glance revealed the fact that they were *new* boots, and of the finest make!

Mrs Connell was staggered. She ran, following a new inspiration, to the coat which he had just hung up. That coat was new likewise—yes, and more marvelous than all, it was lined with good, warm sheepskin!

'Andy Connell,' cried she, 'have you done a robbery? Oh, that ever I married such a man. He's been and done a murder and a robbery. The papers'll be full of it. I ain't gunna be able to lift my head like a honest woman the rest of my days. Andy Connell, how'd you get out here without bein' in the mud?'

Andy, through all of this hubbub, had been calmly warming his hands at the stove. Now he covered a yawn.

'I drove out,' said he. 'Reach me that old pipe of mine, Red, will you? Yonder on the

50

window sill?'

Red obediently brought the pipe. His heart was filled with tenderness for this hounded man, no matter if Connell were a lazy loafer. The burning truth remained that he was a henpecked man, and, as such, the heart of Red warmed to him.

'Mr Connell,' said he, 'when you leave, I'll be goin' along with you. Might be, I could be useful to you?'

Mr Connell peered down at him. 'Son,' said he, 'would you go along with an old beggar like me?'

'In a minute,' said Red with warmth.

Mrs Connell had run to the door. 'Lord love my home,' cried she, and threw up her hands. 'Look!' she added, and summoned the boys.

What they saw was a fine pair of bay mares hitched to a stout road wagon.

'He stole the rig of the gent that he murdered,' groaned Mrs Connell. 'Lewis— look yonder. Ain't that a rider that's comin' here? Ain't that a rider comin' over the hill? No, but they'll be comin' soon. Oh,' she cried, turning on her husband, 'you mighty fool!'

But the last and greatest shock of all was reserved for Mrs Connell. Turning from this denunciation of her husband's rascality, she found that he had actually seated himself by the stove, filled and lighted his pipe, and having made himself perfectly at ease, manlike, by sliding down on the end of his spine and spreading his legs wide, he was blowing leisurely puffs of smoke at the ceiling.

'Connell!' gasped out she.

'Red,' said the prospector, 'they's a day's paper in my coat pocket. You might reach it to me. Doggoned if this here cold mornin' wind ain't stiffened me up a pile!'

'Andrew!' shrilled his wife, with a sudden new tone in her voice.

'Thanks,' said Connell to Red. 'And now my specs on that shelf—you're a mighty handy boy, Red!'

Mrs Connell stood in the center of the floor. Her heart was shaken with a hope so great that it was terrible; it was like fear.

'Andrew Connell,' said she at last, 'as they's a God above me, you must of come into some money.'

Blackie had uncoiled himself from his pleasant seat and now he, also, stood forth with a lean look and an anxious eye.

'Well, Red,' said Connell, looking over the upper rim of his glasses at the youngster, 'they been usin' you tolerable hard around here, I guess?'

Mrs Connell, with a stout hand, threw Red out of the way. 'Andrew,' said she, 'you're breakin' my heart.'

He smiled at her, and the smile was wonderfully close to a sneer. 'What kind of a fool d'you think I might be, Rica?' said he. 'After you been usin' me the way that you have for all of these years, do I aim to think that anything I could do would break your heart?'

He said this with such an air of indifference and of dignity that Red gaped at him. The man seemed new made. As for Mrs Connell, all of her masculinity departed from her. She threw up her hands and collapsed into a chair.

'Here,' moaned she, 'is what money does to a man. He's got rich, and now he ain't got no more need for a wife to be takin' care of him, slavin' for him, cookin' his meals, mendin' his clothes. The back door is good enough for her, now. Him and his fine hosses and his stylish boots—he'll be off to town and let his wife by the law go beggin' and starvin' through the country. Little he'll care!' She burst into a convulsive sobbing. And tears stood in the eyes of Red.

'Mrs Connell,' cried he, 'he ain't gunna treat you as bad as all that.'

She gathered Red to her and wept upon his shoulder. 'Ah, lad,' cried she, 'in the hard times we find the good hearts and the bad ones!'

'He's tol'able foolish,' chuckled Blackie, approaching Mr Andrew Connell with a wink. 'Look how quick she's took him in?'

'Ay,' grinned Andy. 'The girls will make a fool of that boy. He ain't got the head to stand up ag'in 'em, I guess. But I can see by the look of your eye, Blackie, that you ain't no blockhead. You'd see through to the sneakin', treacherous hearts of 'em!'

53

CHAPTER SEVEN

SQUARE WITH HIMSELF

The wind, which had been gathering force for some time, now struck the side of the house a determined cuff that had in it a rattle of rain—hard-driven drops that clicked like metal against the window. Mr Connell, shrinking from this stroke of the hand of winter, hastily drew forth a pint flask and tipped it to his lips. His wife forgot her own grief at this sight.

'Andy! Andy!' cried she. 'You ain't beginnin' *that* ag'in? Better for you a mighty lot if you never *seen* money, if it's gunna make you start in with whisky ag'in!'

Mr Connell, instead of answering, contented himself with scowling upon her while he patted the cork of the bottle home again. Then he reached for the cup of water which Blackie, with great presence of mind, had hastily filled and brought to him. He sipped this chaser, cleared his throat, and settled deeper into the chair with a shrug of his shoulders.

'Well,' said he, 'a gent can be sort of comfortable even in bad weather if he's got some of the summer bottled up, like this. Will you have a mite of it, Blackie?'

'Thanks,' said Blackie, looking not at the bottle, but into the face of Mr Connell. 'I dunno that I'll have any, thanks.'

He was rewarded by an instant smile.

'You got a good head on your shoulders, lad,' said the prospector. 'The stuff ain't right for no kids. It takes a growed-up man and a hardy one, like me, to handle the red eye.'

'Andy,' cried his wife, 'when was you ever able to stand that—' The last words of her sentence were lost in the fresh outbreak of the storm. The rain began to rush in long, slanting volleys out of the sky.

'Them hosses,' said Mr Connell, 'will have to be put up. I'll be back in a minute. And—'

'*I'll* put 'em up!' volunteered Blackie.

Red had started into his coat automatically the instant the rain began, and he was already halfway to the door, when he said: 'I'll handle them hosses.'

'They's a skittish pair,' said the prospector. 'Ain't likely that a kid like you, Red, could handle 'em. Needs a boy with a head on his shoulders—like Blackie, here. A young feller that can't see through a woman, he ain't got no chance to see through the mind and the ways of a hoss. But you might go along and help.'

So the two went through the door together. But it was Red, after the pair had been untethered, who gathered up the reins and drove the span to the shed. There they unharnessed the team, admiring the fine make of the buggy, and the exquisite workmanship of that fine harness.

'Must of cost him a sight,' said Blackie, with a critical eye. 'He must have money to *throw* away, Red.'

'Maybe,' said Red, 'and I guess you aim to have him throw a pile of it your way?'

'Why not?' snapped out Blackie. 'Maybe *you* wouldn't do the same thing, if you could?'

'I wouldn't,' said Red promptly. 'Maybe I'm poor, but I ain't so mighty hard up that I'd beg. Not me!'

'Huh!' snorted Blackie. 'It ain't no use. The old man don't like you, to-day.'

'Because why?'

'Because you acted like a fool when she started in snivelin'.'

'Blackie,' said the other, 'I've seen a mighty lot of you, and they ain't no way that I like you. The way I figger it, you're crooked, clean crooked—all the way to the ground, crooked! They ain't nothin' about you that's straight. You couldn't talk honest no more'n a snake could wriggle straight. You been lyin' and actin' up to old Mrs Connell all this while. The minute Mr Connell comes back, dog-goned if you don't jump over to his side when you seen that he was the strongest of the pair of 'em ag'in. How d'you figure that out to be square?'

Blackie smiled with the scorn which is born of superior knowledge of the conscious sort.

'Look here,' said Red, 'suppose that we fight, and you try to lick me with your fists, how does it make you feel inside when you find that you ain't gunna beat me with your hands and you gotta take a club to me?'

'It means that I pretty near got you turned out of the house,' chuckled Blackie. 'That's what it means for one thing.'

He sat on the edge of the manger, swinging his heels, and watching Red carefully tether the horses to the manger and then fork down some hay for them. The cold wind through which they had passed to the barn had whipped the color into his cheeks. And with his flashing eyes and his cleanly chiseled features, he might have posed for the statue of some young god, some vagrant to the earth in an irreverent century. But Red had none of this rarity about him. Such men as he had lived in every age.

Having ended his work, Red climbed down from the manger. He went fearlessly up to the head of one of those high-strung, nervous horses, too excited by stranger handling and strange quarters to eat. But under the touch of the boy's fingers, he was subdued. Presently he began to munch his fodder. Red, in the meantime, was saying seriously: 'Would you really rather have run me out of the house than have beat me fair and square with your fists?'

'Sure,' said Blackie. 'I hope *I* ain't a fool.'

'Well,' sighed Red, 'some day I'm gunna fight you fair and square. And I'm gunna lick you so's you'll never forget it. I could do it now!'

'You lie!' flashed Blackie, but he cast an

57

apprehensive glance toward the door, and then saw that retreat was impossible. 'Besides,' he went on hastily, 'you wouldn't dare to. The old man would throw you out.'

'Nope. If I licked you, it'd sicken him with you. He ain't the kind that likes a boy that another boy could beat, I guess.'

The truth of this remark turned young Blackie white.

'But,' continued Red, scanning the effect of his last speech with care, 'even if I was to beat you up, Blackie, it wouldn't satisfy me none. I been thinkin' it all over. I don't want to beat you now. It wouldn't mean nothin'. You're weak from bein' inside so much. But when I get you all strong and right up to yourself, then I'm gunna corner you, some day, and pretty near kill you. I'm gunna fight you, Blackie, till you come crawlin' to me, and you beg me to quit because I'm a better man than you are!'

This he said, speaking slowly and with a deliberate care, as one who would not exaggerate anything that he was saying.

'I'd die first!' said Blackie. But still he was sick and white, and his staring eyes seemed to vision the horror of the realization of that same prophecy, however far it might be delayed. Ordinarily, it was hard for Red to look into the eyes of Blackie. For in the eye of Blackie there was ever a working judgment, a working thought, a hidden mockery which baffled Red. Now, however, he looked him through and

58

through and his square jaw set, like a young bulldog.

They went back to the house in apparent amiability, side by side. And on the way Blackie said: 'The old man is gunna go under with the booze, pretty soon. That was what give him the nerve to stand up to the old woman, and he'll keep on at it. He'll keep right on drinkin', for fear that he might lose his nerve ag'in. I know his way!'

He chuckled as he spoke, but Red shivered with a sudden horror.

CHAPTER EIGHT

WHISKY FUMES CONTROL

Just as they stepped through the kitchen door, the bottom was torn out of the rain-filled sky, and the water began to crash on the earth like a cannonade—a sound so appalling and attended with such force that the ground and the whole house quivered until some glassware in a cupboard began to jingle like faint bells.

A dispute which was under way between man and wife was broken off short at this noise of thunder, and they all ran to the windows. The surface of the ground was covered with the white of spray as the thick and heavy drops smashed to bits and recoiled. Every footprint in the mud was instantly turned into a gray pool, then into the source of a small rivulet. Down the valley, they saw a bridge, spanning a torrential mountain stream, lifted and heaved from its place, and then settle again upon the banks as the first head of the uproar leaped away to make new ruin.

After this, the four turned from the windows and looked at one another, blankly, as though, for an instant, they wondered that men could be worrying one another when such calamities were sweeping across the face of the world, within the view of their eyes. However, no sooner was the noise of the tumult passed than it was more than half forgotten. Mr Connell returned to the theme of his last talk, which was the grave abuse of his wife. The presence of the two boys seemed to make no difference to them.

'All right,' said Connell, 'me bein' up on my luck, and partners with such a fine gent and a rich man like old Crawley, you marries me. Ain't that so?'

'Not for your money!' cried the indignant Mrs Connell. 'You didn't have a penny even then.'

'For the hopes of what I would have, though. Me bein' in with "Lucky" Crawley, you aimed to think what the others thought— that I'd be a millionaire pretty pronto. Well, sir, it didn't turn out none too well. Crawley died sudden. He left me some debts and nothin' else. And I had to go bankrupt on account of 'em!'

'The skunk!' murmured Mrs Connell, with a sob.

'That was the beginning of my hard times,' said Connell. 'Nobody had no faith in me after that. They blamed everything onto me. My bad luck was too much for Crawley's good luck, they all said. Except that you said it was because I was a fool.'

'I never said—' shrilled she.

'Don't go raisin' your voice at me!' thundered Mr Connell at the top of his lungs. 'I don't aim to have it told to me what you said or what you didn't. I aim to remember well enough for myself!'

His wife could not answer. She was choked with rage.

'And when you seen that you couldn't squeeze no money out of me, after all, then you turned in and started to make my home into a hell for me. Ain't that the fact?'

'No!' screamed Mrs Connell. 'Andy Connell, how kin you sit there and look your conscience in the face and say that I ain't slaved and—'

'The devil!' said Connell. 'Are you startin' in that yarn ag'in?'

'Listen to me,' he continued, turning to the boys. 'What sort of a home was it that you found that I had here? How was I welcomed back to it, me after bein' so long away?'

61

'With a flatiron at your head,' chuckled Blackie. 'It was a fine home, all right. I could say that in court.'

'You sneakin' traitor!' shrieked Mrs Connell. 'Oh, if I had your gizzard in my hands, I'd wring it out of you, you little, grinnin', lyin', treacherous, hand-lickin'—'

But here the burly prospector pushed between. With one strong hand, turned to iron by long handling of the double-jack, he gathered both of her stout wrists. His pressure ground the flesh against the bone and made her cry out.

'Andy!' she screamed. 'He's killin' me!'

Help came from an unexpected quarter. Red rushed between them like a small fury. One stout young fist beat against the chest of Connell. A blue, Irish devil flamed in the eyes of the boy.

'You bullyin' coward!' he cried. 'Are you handlin' a *woman* like this here?'

Liquor had cast a haze across the mind of Mr Connell, but his brain was still sensible enough to hear the pain in the outcry of his wife. Shame made him loosen his grip. But shame is a bad master for a man. It makes him hate himself and wish to destroy all who have witnessed his debasement. And here was a victim at hand on whom he could expend the wrath which was in his soul.

'I'll learn you manners!' he shouted. 'You red-headed brat.'

And with the full force of his fist, he struck the boy heavily in the face. It snapped his head back like a whiplash swung by a strong hand. And he dropped and would have fallen, had not Mrs Connell received the weight of his body and raised it.

And all that was good in her nature came suddenly to the surface, as she felt that strong young body turned helpless in her arms. Her very voice was calmed as she said to her husband: 'Andrew Connell, has it come to this here, that a poor mite of a boy has got to keep you from beatin' your wedded wife?'

As for Connell, he was stunned. He had in his heart, as strongly as any whole-souled man, a vast disdain of those who take advantage of their own strength to bully the weak.

'Rica,' said he, 'I'm done. I've seen you year in and year out and I ain't seen no good from you yet. Get out of the house and take the brat with you. I'll do without you fine. Me and Blackie'll get along, eh, boy? I'll keep you. I'll pay your way. But outside of money, you'll get nothin' out of me after this day!'

He took out his wallet, balled a few bills into a lump, and hurled them at Mrs Connell. She, for her part, was not so far carried away by fear or by grief, that she did not grasp the proffered coin readily enough, and with Red staggering beside her, she started from the room. At the door, she turned and looked back.

'They'll be a day,' she said prophetically,

'when you'll wish to Heaven that you'd taken a snake into your house sooner'n that young rat, Andy Connell, and mark my word for it. I've seen the inside of him. And he's poison, every bit!'

So she left the room and tramped up the stairs, leaving Andy Connell with his chin sunk upon his breast.

Looking back upon her life, it seemed to Mrs Connell that no martyr had ever suffered more, or more causelessly. Such a transformer of the truth is persecution.

In the meantime, therefore, it would be well to go to the town, collect a little sympathy from the townsfolk, pass on to the city, and there hire a lawyer to take charge of her affairs. For, if there were a divorce before her, there was also such a thing as alimony, and lawyers knew how to collect it.

But what if, after all, her husband had not really come upon a fortune of any size? In that case it would be best to stay close at home and collect what she could in that fashion. In the first place, she must count what money he had given her.

She spread out the bills one by one. There were only five, and the denomination of the first was a dollar!

Mrs Connell, with a gasp of indignation, cast the offensive bit of paper to the ground and snatched up a second. But at this, she almost swooned away. For it was a fifty-dollar bill—a fifty-dollar bill in the hands of Andy Connell! How could such a thing have come to pass?

She stared at the third, and blood swam across her eyes. It was for a hundred. And beneath it was another century note. The last blow was the greatest shock of all. For it called for five hundred dollars, payable to the bearer by the treasury of the United States.

Mrs Connell began to pack, and as she packed, Red recovered. He stood up from the bed. He went with uncertain steps around the room, and fumbled with his numbed fingers at a lump on the side of his head where the hard fist of Mr Connell had struck him. He was still more than half at sea, but he was enough for Mrs Connell to use as an audience to her monologue.

The tide of sorrow, of wounded pride, of fiery indignation by turns mastered the bosom of Frederica Connell.

'Here I am,' she wailed, 'growin' old fast— nigh forty-five my last birthday and now turnin' gray and gettin' feeble. Here I am without no children to help me, turned out—'

The stunned brain of Red cleared another bit. 'I'll be a help to you, Mrs Connell,' he said loyally.

He did not like Mrs Connell. There was nothing about her that appealed to him except her unusual neatness. But everything else was not as he would have it in woman. However, his devotion was not to Mrs Frederica Connell, but to the whole abstract idea of downtrodden women, who must be rescued to the full ability of all able-bodied men—or boys.

His proffer was not kindly received, however.

'*You'll* be a help!' cried Mrs Connell. 'Lord knows that if it hadn't been for you, I'd still be in this house as the lady of it and the wife of the richest man in Turner County! But you had to step in between us, you little red-headed, ignorant—Oh, Oliver Hardwick, you've brought bad luck into this house. Heaven forgive you for it!'

'Ma'am,' said Red slowly, 'I dunno how I'm to blame. But I guess I am. Is there any law how he can throw you out of his house?'

'What law does the great brute want?' she cried. She held forth her two stout wrists. They were banded about with red circles.

In the meantime, all was quiet in the kitchen of the house. Mr Connell had made an oration to Blackie in which, in the first place, he held forth upon the wicked weakness of all women and in which, in the end, he condemned, above all, the wickedness of his wife. In the midst of the latter part of this oration, he fell into a sound slumber.

Blackie had listened, nodding, grinned, and showing his approbation in every way he could to this speech; but when it ended, and when he saw the big prospector subdued in sleep, he

66

rose from his own place with a look of resolution combined with fear. Like a mouse he moved, which knows the trap and dreads it, but is overpowered by the smell of the toasted cheese within.

So it was with Lewis Jason.

First, as he stood up stealthily, he examined the figure of the sleeper with care, to see how much of this sleep might be feigned. But it was apparently a true stupor.

Andrew Connell was sagged far back in the chair, his legs sprawling, his head dropped far over his right shoulder. One hand lay palm up on his knee. The other hung inert toward the floor. Such a position could not have been maintained long by any actor without some stir, and there was no quiver in the big body of Connell.

So Lewis Jason crossed the room toward the coat of Connell which he had hung there on a peg. He crossed it by moving backward, still with his fascinated eye fixed upon the sleeper. He reached the coat, he slid a trembling hand into the side pocket and brought forth the wallet.

It was stoutest pigskin. Now time and wear had turned it into a rich brown-black, so often seen in old saddles. And it bulged with fatness. The thick, soft feel of it made the eyes of Blackie start with greed. He opened it, and first he saw a number of yellowed papers in a side pocket. Next, in the two main compartments

67

of the wallet, he found thick sheafs of money.

His trembling fingers, too, made the task doubly difficult. But he worked the bills apart and counted. Mostly, the bills were of large denominations. He passed the hundreds. He entered the thousands, with his mind reeling with joy. Two, three, four thousand! And this was only half the treasure.

Here were Mrs Connell and Red about to leave the house. Here was the owner, dead drunk. Suppose that he should simply put that wallet into his pocket, pass through the door, and fade away among the hills? It might be hours before the prospector wakened. It might be days before, in this stormy weather, the thief's trail could be located across the mountains. Yet, because of its very simplicity, Blackie hesitated. He was too canny to take such a long step without regarding all of the consequences. Better, perhaps, to put the wallet back and ponder the matter from all sides and in all lights before he made the theft. There was time.

He had turned and put the wallet back into its proper pocket before he heard something breathing in the room. Was it the sound of the wind? Wind never caused such regularly rhythmical noises. Moreover, the sound approached him!

He whirled about, and there he saw Andy Connell risen from his chair, and gliding forward with a terribly, swollen, purple face, and one hand stretched forth with the fingers stiff to clutch. Blackie, frozen with dread, could not stir.

He could barely speak and say: 'Your coat fell down, Mr Connell. I thought I'd pick it up—'

'Ah!' snarled out Connell, and leaped the rest of the way upon the boy.

'You liar and traitor!' gasped Connell. 'You been fingerin' my money!'

He took Blackie by the nape of the neck and swung him around. The band of his shirt caught his throat and well-nigh choked him. Black swam before his eyes. Then he was slammed against the wall. Over him stood Connell with a demoniac face; and his whisky breath beat against the boy.

'You can search me!' moaned Blackie, blinking his eyes, for he expected the mortal blow to be delivered at any instant.

Connell, fumbling for the throat with his other hand, paused and repeated the thought thickly.

'Search you?' said he. 'Meanin' that you ain't got none of it? Well, boy, I kind of half think that you ain't. You wouldn't of dared. Not with me in the room so near. Go get me the coat!'

He flung Blackie halfway across the room, and Blackie came back with the coat, with his brain whirling, wondering how it chanced that he was still living. The prospector took the coat and jerked the wallet from it. He opened it, made sure that the two sheafs were there, and dropped back into his chair, more than half sobered with his shock.

'Well, Blackie, you ain't gunna regret it none. I'm gunna be like a father to you. I'm gunna take care of you. I'm gunna give you a home and a rearin', and a trainin'. I'm gunna show that Red what he missed. Why, Blackie, I could of loved that there boy. I could of loved him, and here he turns around and tries to make me hate him. There's gratitude for you.'

Maudlin tears poured into his eyes.

'They's no place in the world for a man that means good,' he said. 'They's no place at all. But, Blackie, you ain't gunna ride on nothin' but thoroughbreds from now on. You're gunna go to the best school in this here country. You're gunna be taught mighty smooth manners. You're gunna be the kind that folks say: "There's a gentleman born and bred!" And what'll you think when they say that? You'll think: "Here am I, Lewis Jason, and old man Connell; he found me and he picked me up out of the dirt and he made me everything that I am right now." That's what you're gunna say. And you're gunna call me father. Yes, sir, I'll have a right to be called that. I'm gunna drive into town and make you my son and heir. I can do anything. I got money. I got gold. I can dig it right out of the rocks, all the gold that I can use—more'n all I
70

can use. We're both rich. We got millions—millions, Blackie. Gimme that flask, and then go harness up that team!'

CHAPTER NINE

BROKEN BRIDGES

Down the stairs of the house Mrs Connell moved with a slow and dragging step. At every step she paused to complain.

'Oh, I wish I'd never been born. It was all because of you comin' between me and my husband, Oliver Hardwick. D'you think that I needed any protection? Me? Ain't I stood up to him twenty times before?'

'Lemme carry that grip,' suggested Red patiently. For back in his mind was lodged an old precept, that it was useless to argue with women, and irritating. So he endured this abuse with no attempt at a rejoinder.

At the door of the kitchen Mrs Connell thrice started ahead and thrice paused, and at last she pushed open the door slowly, and peered inside. She saw her husband seated at the table, the nearly emptied flask beside him and his face dark with a steady scowl as he stared straight back at her.

'Andrew Connell,' she quavered, 'I hope that God forgives you, as I do.'

71

He made no reply. He sat like a stone.

'May you get richer 'n richer!' she sobbed. 'God knows that I don't wish you nothin' but good! I ain't beggin' you to take me back. It's the love for you that makes me mighty sad, Andy, dear!'

'Woman,' he cried in a fury, 'I ain't gunna talk with you. If I had a pair of tongues, it wouldn't be no good in me tryin' to talk back to you! No good at all!' He stood up and banged his fist on the table. 'Git out and don't lemme see your face no more!'

Mrs Connell did not hesitate. There was that in the countenance of her spouse which she had never seen there before, and now she shrank back through the doorway and ran out of the house, across the graveled path, and to the road where, at the first step, she sank above the ankles in the mud.

'Heaven love me!' cried Mrs Connell. 'We'll never get to the town. It'll be the death of me, Red!'

But Red, following more slowly with her bag, said not a word. He slogged slowly down the road, silent, head down, heart-heavy. His head was still ringing with the terrific blow which Andrew Connell had struck him. But his heart was far more heavy than his head. He was trying to piece this matter together and put it to rights. A boy loves logic. And what he detests most in the world is the absence of fair play. In such a case as this, from a man whom he had proven in the past to be gentle and open-minded, he could not understand the reverse of nature.

Only one thing could account for it. That was the whisky. It had subdued all that was good in the prospector and left him, for the moment, a sheer brute.

They had almost reached the point where the road touched the ravine, still deep with wildly rushing water which raised a roar louder than a shouting human voice. Now they could see how the bridge had been struck. Half the width of the road it had been pushed to the side, yet it lay level enough, though they could see that one of the big side beams which supported it had been broken quite in two.

Red had to touch the arm of Mrs Connell to warn her to get out of the way, for she could not hear his voice. They turned in time to see Andrew Connell sweep past them in his new buggy, the pair of young horses striking bravely out in spite of the mud, which flew from the wheels like fire from a spin wheel.

In the seat Andrew Connell had a strong grip on the reins and, with his pipe gripped hard and tilted at a sharp angle, his eyes flashing with the joy of the speed, his head bare, his gray hair flying, he sent the horses faster and faster ahead. Beside him was Blackie, the hat of his adopted father-to-be in his lap, and his back straight with pride. He laughed exultantly at the pair in the mud as they flashed past. He

73

even turned to wave to them. And at that instant the team struck the bridge.

At the first impact of the strong hoofs the whole fabric swayed sickeningly. And the instant that the entire weight of horses and buggy rested on the bridge, it buckled and crashed into the water.

The buggy flew into kindling wood at the impact. Blackie, unable to clutch the seat rail for support, was thrown lightly out of the rig and into the brush on the farther bank of the stream, while the horses, kicking furiously to rid themselves of the wreckage, were presently free and started wildly to the same shore.

But the buggy itself, or the tangled remains of it, with Andrew Connell in their midst, was now in the sweep of the upper waters of the stream, which combed furiously across the sunken middle section of the bridge, and the moment the horses were free, the buggy and Connell with it was swept down into the full, deep force of the stream.

It left Mrs Connell stunned, until at last she threw up her hands to the sky, and shook them in a fury of excitement.

'It's the act of God!' cried Mrs Connell. 'There's his reward for drivin' his wife out of his house. God forgive him and save him! Red, Red, do somethin' to help him.'

Red had not waited for that call. The instant the crash came instinct drove him forward, that controlling instinct in his nature which always sent him headlong toward the point of the first danger. He ran toward the wreckage, saw Connell swept into the little river, and accordingly turned and raced down the bank beside the form of Connell.

Twice he saw the latter whirled past outthrusting stumps of logs. Twice he himself turned in, filled with a desperate resolve to get to the endangered man.

Fast as the river ran, he could go far faster. But what would that avail the poor swimmer? Even skill in swimming was poor aid to Connell. Desperately he struck out, and all of his force strove to keep his head above the water, but the river was a thing of a thousand contrary hands. Now it tossed him to the surface. Now it dragged him down again. Now it whirled him over and over.

There was a louder shouting of the water just ahead of him, a place where the stream leaped down a hundred yards of rapids, ordinarily trickling gently enough among the big boulders, but now broken into a dashing white water in which nothing could have lived for an instant.

But the danger held forth a hope, also. For at the edge of the rapids there were large stones which thrust out of the water sometimes a foot, sometimes a few inches. And Red formed the hazardous determination of working into midstream from stone to stone, taking his chance of being whipped downstream by the current

75

which drove through the interstices.

He was away in a flash. On the edge of the bank opposite the edge of the rapids, he cast one sickened glance down the yelling white water. Then he stepped into the creek. The very first steps told him something of what was coming. For though this was the shallow, where water would be comparatively still, yet now it dragged at him like stiff mud as he waded out.

He was up to the waist at once, and now his progress was extremely hazardous. He had to feel with foot and hand for each rock and stone on his right, get a grip or a foothold, and then make another forward step. Once his handhold failed, and he was shot down the gulf between two rocks, hurled by the rush of smooth-sliding water.

He found by luck a rough place on the same rock which had failed him, and by it first stopped his fall to destruction, then drew himself back behind the broken barrier of stones.

He was nearly breast deep, now, and the force of the stream sent a curling ripple up to his chin. But at least he had succeeded in putting himself fairly in the way of Andrew Connell as the latter flailed his way down the creek.

Connell had spent the first of his great strength in attempting to get from the grip of the midstream to the shallows; but that effort had failed, and now he was letting himself drift straight down to the rapids and to the certain death which waited for him there. For, driving at such a speed, there was not a chance in a thousand that he could fasten his grip on one of those slippery, jutting rocks—far greater chance that they would merely serve to break his head or his arms as he gripped at them.

He came fast. Now he saw Red, and he was not too far away for the boy to see the wild flash of hope that gleamed on his face, lifted that moment well away from the surface. He raised an arm as a signal that he saw and understood; and at that instant a drifting log, driven forward by a boiling water from behind, lunged straight across the body of Connell.

Red closed his eyes, half sickened. When he looked again, the log was whipped past him through the throat of the nearest water shoot between the rocks. But there was no sight of Connell. Yes, here he came, wonderfully close, a few inches beneath the water, floating sidewise, limp and helpless.

Straight at him came the swept body of Connell. Then, at the last instant, a side current jerked it away and straight into the throat of the nearest flume. Only by the heel did Red fasten his grip. The body was torn half through his fingers. Then his grip held, one hand on the foot of Connell, one hand fastened on the rock, and the pull made his shoulders ache, as though his arms were in danger of being plucked out by the roots. He closed his eyes. He could not pray, for all his mind was a blackness and an agony of effort. There was only one thought, and that was the thought of the bulldog as it fastens its grip.

Then, in a jerk, the water relaxed its pressure, the body of Connell came easily in to him, and a moment later one hand was around the body of the man, holding his head above the water, and with the other arm gripping the rock.

It was a dead face which lay so close to his, with the water foaming around it. The eyes were closed. The face was white and haggard. And crimson ran from a rip across the forehead. He was as far as ever from making a rescue. Certainly, though he had halted the sweep of the stream for the moment, he could never hope to wade back through the current, dragging this inert burden.

His own strength was going like the very race of the water. A wild excitement had sustained him until he had the body in his grip. But now he began to think, and he gave way to despair. If he waited a little longer, it would be impossible for him to wade back to the shore. And yet he could not loosen his hold on Connell, even if the body were that of a corpse.

Here was a possibility of rescue—Blackie on one side of the river and Mrs Connell on the other. But Blackie, after wading in knee-deep, hastily turned and scrambled back again, and

78

Mrs Connell had dropped on her knees, thrown up her arms to God, and then fallen into violent hysterics. There was no salvation in them. If they were saved it must be in their own strength.

Still there was no sign of life in that limp body. He looked up. The scouring wind whirled the rain clouds low across the face of the earth. But the storm was silent, for the bellow of the water-choked ravine drowned all other sound.

His eyes grew dizzy, and with a feeling that his arms could not endure the strain for another moment, he glanced down to Connell again. He could not comprehend, at first, for the eyes were open. And then he recalled that the dying open their eyes when death itself comes. No, for the lids stirred—and the mouth gaped at the air, and now a thick arm, round with mighty muscle, was lifted above the surface of the stream.

He lived! But wounded, perhaps, and helpless? No, no, for now he stood erect, and the water which foamed around the throat of the boy was hardly at the mighty shoulder of the man, and the fight was over.

CHAPTER TEN

TABLES TURNED

At that instant, both of Red's arms grew helpless from shoulder to finger tip, and blackness shot across his eyes. He fought away that weakness. He looked up, and he saw on the face of the big man such joy and such sweetness of the new taste of life that he was transformed.

He staggered in the sweep of the current, but a great hand took him by the nape of the neck and lifted him forward. Through that perilous race of water past the rocks, Connell strode easily, freely, and came to the farther bank.

Red, like a wet rag, crumpled on the mud, for Connell was leaning above his wife and raising her to her feet. It was characteristic of her that she forgot the last danger the instant that it was past.

'Andy, Andy,' she sobbed. 'It's the red eye that brung you to this.'

And he answered her quietly: 'It ain't the liquor. It was the money. I was drunk with gold. I was drunk with havin' more'n I could use—Heaven hear me swear it—I'll never spend on myself ag'in more'n enough to hold body and soul together! Rica, take hold on Red, he's plumb spent. We're all goin' home together.'

*   *   *

Nothing of this conversation was heard by Red. His ears were too filled with water and the roar of the stream, and his mind was too shadowed by all that had passed. But, most of all, his body was utterly spent. The last scruple of his power had been drained from him in the river. When Mrs Connell laid hold of him, it was like laying hold of a helpless infant. He had not fainted, but when he tried to stand, his legs buckled under him.

When they reached the road, Blackie was there to join them, a wonderfully transformed Blackie, full of solicitation concerning the injured boy, offering to help carry half of his weight.

'Keep behind me!' said big Andrew Connell. 'I don't like the look of your face. If I ever seen a rat, I see one now!'

Blackie, at this harsh address, fell obediently to the rear, but he did not fail to follow. He went in the deepest thought. He had been sitting on a burning throne of golden expectations, a little moment before. They were half snatched from him, now, but not entirely. So great a hope does not pass suddenly.

So he trailed up the weary, muddy way. They reached the house, and there he sat in a corner of the kitchen while Andy Connell ripped the wet clothes from the body of Red and wrapped him in a blanket, and while Mrs Connell hurried back and forth, kindling a roaring fire, preparing hot tea.

Red lay on the bed in the adjoining room, and Blackie could hear his voice, after a time, raised to a shrill, unaccustomed pitch, babbling constantly, steadily, words which had no meaning. The white and frightened face of Andrew Connell, rendered hideous by the red stains which had dried and blackened on his face, but which was left unheeded there, appeared in the doorway.

'His head is burnin' hot. He's talking stuff with no sense. Rica, he's gone batty sure! He's gone nutty, Rica!'

'You talk like a fool!' cried Mrs Connell. 'He ain't no more'n delirious. He's plumb fagged and sort of shook up. He'll pull together—but sort of slow. Go get a doctor, Andy. Go over to Doc Jerney's house quick!'

Away rushed Andy Connell, hatless, desperate, and came back in an hour with the doctor. Doctor Jerney heard the story, and spent five minutes with Red.

'It's shock,' he said when he came out. 'He'll come through well enough. He used himself up. There's no strength inside him, now. If he has the proper treatment—'

'He'll have it—oh, he'll have it,' muttered big Connell. 'You go to town. You get the best

82

nurses you can find. You buy everything that's needed, and all the delicate sort of food—'

'Connell,' said the doctor in some impatience, 'you must remember, man, that I have other patients.'

From his wallet Connell extracted a bill. That it was for five hundred dollars made no difference to him, though it made a vast difference to the doctor.

'You got *no* other patients!' he shouted. 'You ain't got a thing to do except to take care of this here boy until he gets well. Fix him up and I'll make you comfortable for life. Let him die and I'll murder you, Jerney.'

The doctor rolled his eyes, pocketed the money, and then fled.

It was all strange to Blackie. Sometimes, bitterly, he wished that *he* had plunged into the stream and made the rescue. But then he called up the picture of the danger, and he knew that he never could have done it.

Besides, Red might die!

It was late that night before any one took any notice of him, and then Connell leaned above him and said: 'You ain't left yet?'

'I ain't left,' said Blackie. 'I thought that you might have a need for me.'

'Me?' said Connell sneeringly. 'A need for *you?*'

It was a shock, but Blackie had braced himself for it. 'A gent usually has some sort of use for his adopted son,' he said.

'Damnation!' cried Connell. 'I ain't adopted you.'

'You've swore that you would, though,' answered Blackie. 'You put up your hand like you was in court and you swore that you would.'

Connell, remembering, blinked hard. Then he nodded. 'This here is my punishment,' he said at last. 'This here is to remind me of what I come near doin'. I got to have you for a son. You! What stood on the bank and let Red jump in to help me, and him after I'd knocked him down for nothin'—good Lord, it's a mighty funny world.'

He added: 'Keep clear of me to-day, Blackie. Maybe I can stand the sight of you to-morrow.'

Blackie started slowly for the door, and as he went he heard the prospector murmuring: 'And fine clothes, and a gold watch and a good schoolin' like a gentleman—I remember it all. It's my punishment.'

Hearing that, Blackie stole away, contented. As for the love and the pride, he would do without that. A little hard cash was the great difference to him!

Connell went back into the room of Red. There he remained day by day, night by night. His beard stood rank and gray on his face. His eyes grew hollow and bloodshot. But he sat by the bedside and watched Red grow more wan, more white, more deadly thin. It didn't seem as if he could live.

84

There were two nurses in white clothes. They came and went, and Andy Connell was unaware of them. There was his wife who passed into the room and out again. But Andy Connell saw her not. There was the doctor who called three times a day in all weathers, but Andy Connell saw nothing; he heard nothing, it seemed to him, from the moment he brought Red to the shore to the moment when Red opened his eyes and looked up to him from beneath puckered brows.

'How might it be goin' with you?' said Connell, frightened by the strangeness of those eyes.

'I disremember—everything!' said Red, and went to sleep.

'He ain't gunna have no mind left him,' whispered Connell to the doctor that night. 'God pity you if he ain't!' And he balled his great fist in a fury.

But the next morning Red opened his eyes and yawned. 'Jiminy,' said he. 'I'm hungry.'

Andy Connell tried to speak and could not. So he got up and stumbled into the kitchen and stood at the open door until the winter wind had calmed him.

Then: 'Rica,' he said, 'our boy is askin' for chuck. Go feed him.'

CHAPTER ELEVEN

CONNELL KEEPS HIS WORD

When they returned to the lawyer's office, Connell gave the reins to Blackie and told him to hold the team until he came back. Then he went up to Jeffrey Morgan's office. Even a 'city' lawyer might have been proud of that office. In such a town as Jackson Corners it was palatial. The door, as it opened, whispered over the long-napped carpet which covered the floor with deepest red.

Even a stamped foot was hushed upon that carpet. Out of its shadowy red arose brown-black mahogany, glimmering with dull red high lights—table, desk, chairs, all mahogany. Mr Morgan paused for a moment to enjoy the surprise and the delight of his client, but Connell clumped across the carpet in his boots, leaving sooty smudges of mud wherever he trod; then he dropped into a chair.

Small things hurt the most. A sharp word rose to the throat, to the very teeth of Mr Jeffrey Morgan before he remembered with cautious timeliness that this same rough-hewn fellow had scooped a golden fortune out of the rocks of his little farm not many weeks before. Such a client was not easily won; such a client was not easily to be lost, if Mr Morgan could help it.

'The devil!' said Mr Morgan. 'This wind is increasing. It will be another storm in half an hour.'

The exclamation, mild as it was, relieved him somewhat. And to give point to his remark, he went to the window. Looking down to the street he saw the boy keeping a tight pull on the reins and ducking his head to the gale which came down the street edged with sand. A cow-puncher waddled across the street, leaning sidewise, his bandanna whipped out level over his shoulder.

'Bad weather for a boy to be holding a spirited team like that span, Andy,' said the lawyer.

'Ain't I done enough for that boy to-day, Jeff?' asked the prospector.

The nickname struck the lawyer like a blow in the face, for he was proud of his blood. He was in the first place a Morgan. He was in the next place a Jeffrey. And here was a town 'character' whom the entire district called Andy, and who now presumed upon an old acquaintance and an indefinite quantity of newly acquired money, to call Jeffrey Morgan, 'Jeff.'

But, though Mr Morgan compressed his lips, he relaxed them again. He answered the question of Connell.

'You have done a great deal, sir,' he said. 'I presume that when a man has given a boy his

87

own name and made him his heir, he can hardly be expected to do more.'

'Then, darn him,' said Connell, 'let him do something for me and hold my horses in the wind. It's about all I can get out of him.'

Mr Morgan was justly bewildered. For he had at that moment completed the entire legal transaction which had made 'Blackie,' properly known as Lewis Jason, the legal son and heir of Andy Connell, with the right to use the name of Connell as his own. This done, and certainly there appeared no reason for it other than the bigness of the heart of Connell and the greatness of his love for the boy, the demeanor of the prospector might be called very odd indeed.

'I'm trying to be guided by the hand of God,' vouchsafed the strange visitor.

But the lawyer's god was his own sharp wits and he waited for the old man to explain the mystery.

'You see,' finally frowned Andy Connell, 'I have had a pretty sharp lesson from the hand of God—a lesson all planned out for the sake of teaching me something I needed to learn.

'First, when I struck gold, I run wild and talk big. I act like *I* was God. And in the middle of me bein' proud, He knocks me down and has me helpless and then what does He do? Why, the thing that'll make me feel the smallest and the meanest. He gives me my life out of the hand of a boy, and a boy that I've wronged!'

He writhed at the thought and struck his big, weather-blackened hands together.

'Was that luck, Jeff?' he cried. 'No, sir, I tell you that I seen and I felt. If you was in that water swirlin' around, you wouldn't stand there and shake your head now! And when I come out, I'd made up my mind that I'd never taste liquor again, and that I'd never spend my money on myself. I was thinkin' of a fine house in a big city, and a pile of servants, and them things. I was thinkin' of a steam yacht—'

'Good heavens, Andy,' cried the lawyer, aghast, 'how much money *have* you dug out of those rocks? We all know that you've struck it rich. But the miners keep their mouths shut, and we don't hear any figures.'

'How much money?' asked the prospector with a rather grim smile. 'I can tell you this much, Jeff. I've took out millions —millions!'

Mr Jeffrey Morgan blinked and sighed. He had been glad to have the patronage of this man on the mere repute that he was taking much coin out of the ground. But at the thought that he had nearly taken a chance of offending an actual millionaire, he grew faint.

'It doesn't seem possible, Andy,' he muttered. 'Millions? How could you take out so much in such a short time? You've had your big operations going at the mine for how long? Only a few weeks, at the most.'

Pleasure filled the eye of the prospector as he filled and tamped and lighted his pipe.

'Well, sir,' he said at last, 'when I found it first, it was like comin' on diamonds by the pocketful. That there gold was lodged in pockets. All that had to be done, first off, was to scoop it out. I done that at first. I come back secret, by night, and cleaned out that surface stuff. How much it come to don't sound likely. But that was only scratchin' the surface. When I come back and turned loose a whole minin' crew of old-timers on that place, they just cracked open a vein and started rakin' it out with both hands. There wasn't no limit to it.

'We've finished the cream. But there's a lot of pickin's left. How deep down that vein'll go, I dunno.'

Jeffrey Morgan perhaps did not agree with a word that he had heard, but when a client had millions, Mr Morgan was willing to transform his private opinions at the first bidding.

'But I cannot quite see how this boy Lewis Jason, Blackie, as you call him, has any claim upon you.'

'After I give him my word that I'd adopt him?' grunted the prospector.

'A promise made in a moment of excitement, to a boy, never would hold in a thousand years in a court as a legal claim against you, Andy.'

Andrew Connell snorted. 'Partner,' he said, 'I ain't takin' no chances. I tell you,' he added with a peculiar combination of pride and of terror in his voice, 'that God is watchin' me pretty close. One slip, and he wipes me out! He sent Red into the river to pull me out and give me one more chance. How else could a boy like Red of done a thing that hardly any growed-up man would have the strength for? No, sir, I was brung back and given another chance. D'you think that I aim to throw that chance away by breakin' a promise that I've swore to?'

The lawyer smiled faintly. 'It may make a man out of him.'

'He's too much of a man already,' snarled out Andy Connell, and rose to leave.

*   *   *

Blackie, in the meantime, had been sorely tried. He had two great difficulties to contend with. One was the handling of that nervous team while the storm wind combed down the street and whipped against his face and blew out his overcoat behind him. The other was the jibing of the little crowd which leaned against the pillars of the store veranda, above which were the law offices of Jeffrey Morgan.

Only with single glances, now and then, he marked down his tormentors and seemed to inscribe them in his memory. Now the leadership was taken by a stalwart youth some years too old for the work, some inches and many pounds too big. A brown-faced hard-fisted stripling who lounged out from the door of the store, took in the situation in a moment, and then joined in the fun.

91

'Who might your pa be, Blackie?' he asked. Blackie for the first time stiffened. But he made no answer. When one's hands are filled with reins, it is better not to need them for other employment at the same time. The newcomer went on, pushing his battered black felt hat far back on his head and chopping his fists upon his hip: 'And who might your ma be, Blackie?'

The voice of Blackie barked out a sudden answer: 'A better and a finer lady than you ever so much as *seen*!'

'What?' shouted the other, stung by the unexpected retort. 'Are you talkin' back to me, you runt? I'll hammer you for that!'

And just at this moment Mr Andrew Connell stepped out from the door which led to the office in the second story. He heard just enough to explain everything, and the thing he did was eloquent of that understanding.

'Blackie,' he said, stepping to the heads of the horses and taking them with a firm grip, 'I'll mind the hosses if you got any errands that need running.'

The fine dark eyes of the boy grew brilliant with hope, with inquiry, as he stared at his newly found father for a moment. In the face of the miner he found all that he wished for. He dropped the reins, and standing up, he stripped off overcoat and coat, sweeping the group of boys who had been persecuting him in the meantime with side glances, as though to select a victim. His coat off, he whirled and leaped from the buggy.

The most chosen tormentor was not at hand. He was too far back. But a second best choice was in the road at the edge of the veranda, and Blackie made him the target. With knees drawn up high and sharp elbows presented, he struck the unlucky boy in a compact ball and sent him crashing against the edge of the porch. The shock rolled Blackie in the mud—it knocked both wind and senses from the other and dropped him in a lifeless heap.

But Blackie was on his feet again. He did not hesitate. Half the battle is won by him who delivers the first and most resolute charge. So Blackie leaped onto the veranda and went at the chief of the village youths. Inches in height and many and many a vital pound in bulk were on the side of the one in the black felt hat. But on the side of Blackie was a consuming passion, a righteous cause, and the science which had enabled him to stand up to Red in many and many a bitter fight. His fists were iron, his muscles were rubber cordage. And at the first blow the black hat leaped into the air, the tousled head of the owner bobbed back. At the second the tall youth doubled over. At the third, he went down in a heap, and Blackie upon him, whining with a tigerish, joyous rage.

They pulled Blackie off before his fingers were well settled in the throat of the second victim. They pulled him off and brought him back to Connell as fast as they could.

93

'Where might the blame be, partner?' asked Connell.

It was an old man and a just one who answered: 'Them that hunt trouble get it. This kid has sand, Connell.'

So thought Andy Connell, though he said not a word until he came to the railroad station and stood on the platform with the boy. The train itself was in sight, a small black front with towering smoke above it in the distance, before he spoke.

'Blackie,' said he, 'you and me are gettin' along to understand each other. They's things about you that I don't like, Blackie, and they's things about me that you don't cotton to. But a boy that's got spunk is a boy that I take to nacheral, you might say. Now, Blackie, I'm sendin' you off to a school where it might be that you'll like things and it might be that you won't. Write to me and tell me how you get on. If things ain't right there for you, let me know. I ain't gunna forget that you're wearin' the name of Connell from now on.'

There was discretion beyond his years in Blackie. And when he took the big proffered hand of the prospector he simply said: 'I've done a pile of wrong things to you, Mr Connell. But I been long enough without a father to put a value on one when I find him. I hope I ain't gunna disgrace your name none, sir.'

So he climbed up the steps to the train and
94

from his seat in the car waved through the window to Connell, and Connell waved back and waited until the train was a disappearing speck down the tracks before he went back to his team.

On his way home, he was thoughtful. Courage, indeed, he liked, and courage was in Blackie. And good looks, and a well-made body, and a quick brain. As for certain failings, they might be outgrown. So reason all mature men concerning boys, never pausing to consider that what the boy is the man will be, and that the souls we inherit at birth are the souls with which we died. They just don't consider the real truth.

In the meantime the fast-stepping trotters brought him up the valley and to the little cabin which served him as a home. On the ridge behind the house yawned the black hole of the mouth of the mine, with little shacks around it in which the workers lived. He looked to it again and again while he unhitched and watered the horses. There was the visible token of the millions which were his. And though he had forsworn the use of money for himself, he could not help taking the relish of that thought keenly on his mind, so to speak.

When he had fed the bays, he went back to the house and found his wife leaning over the stove. She was in a wicked temper and lost no time in showing it.

'There ain't no draft in this here stove, Andy

Connell,' she complained. 'When are you gunna get me a new one?'

He stood over the offending stove for a moment and considered.

'I aim to think this here stove will do for a few years longer,' he said.

'Years?' cried his wife. 'Years? Are you gunna keep me here slavin' for *years* when you got your pockets full of money to burn?'

'Have I?' he grumbled. 'And should I give *you* a match to burn it? And where would you be goin' to do the burnin', Rica?'

She bit her lip to keep from answering. Her problem was a sad one. If she left him in a tantrum, she would get nothing from him, so the lawyer advised her.

Had he become a miser? Surely not, for he had this day sent Blackie away to school equipped with clothes, cash, and all that could be needful in a schoolboy's life. What was the reason for such penury around the house? But she dared not ask too many questions. She must wear a pleasant face and make the best of a very bad matter. Perhaps she would find out in time.

'Where's Red?' asked the miner at last.

'Sittin' up in his room by the window.'

'Sittin' up?' cried Connell. 'He's better, then?'

'A pile, the doctor said this afternoon.'

'By the heavens, I'll make that doctor glad he's on this here earth!' exclaimed Connell.

'He's pulled the kid through. They ain't no doubt of that, Rica!'

'Nacheral meanness and toughness,' suggested his better half with some malice.

Her husband smiled. 'He ain't been sidin' with you, maybe,' said Connell. 'When you been in his room complainin' about me, he ain't took your side, maybe?'

'Andy Connell!' cried she. 'What sort of language are you talkin' at me now?'

But her husband merely shrugged his broad shoulders and went straightway to Red's room.

CHAPTER TWELVE

RED REFUSES A FORTUNE

When Andrew Connell came into his room in the dusk of the day, Red looked up to the uncertain outline of the big man at the door, bulky, huge, misshaped in the darkness.

'Well, kid,' said the man, 'how are you comin'?'

'Pretty fair,' said Red. 'I'm comin' on.'

'Hungry?'

'Like a wolf.'

'That's good. Eatin' is the main cause of gettin' well, I reckon.'

He took a chair and drew it close to the

97

invalid. 'You'll be out rovin' around in a day or two,' said he.

'I reckon,' said Red.

'I seen Blackie off.'

There was silence for a moment. Then, though Red hated Blackie with all of his heart, he forced himself out of justice to say: 'Blackie'll do fine in school. He's smart.'

'He is,' said the prospector. 'He'll take to books pretty fine.' Then he added: 'How about you, Red?'

'Me?'

'About school, you know.'

'Why,' said Red, 'was you aimin'—'

'To send you off?'

'Why, I didn't know—'

'D'you think,' said the big man with emotion, 'that I'd do less for you than I'd do for Blackie?'

'I didn't know,' said Red.

Connell cleared his throat. 'I been waitin' till you was in better shape,' he said, 'so's that you and me could have a talk. And now that you're lookin' up, I can talk, Red, and tell you what I got in my mind. I made a promise to Blackie, and I've lived up to it. I've give him my name to wear. I've made him my son. I've sent him away to school. Now, Red, I'm gunna do the same thing by you!'

'You're gunna put me in school?'

'Would you like that?'

'I'd like that fine!'

'You'll go, then, soon as you can walk around comfortable. But the other thing—'

'What other thing, Mr Connell?'

'The makin' of you into my legal son—the same as Blackie. We got to do that before we send you off.'

So excited was Connell by the swelling of his heart and the sense of his own goodness that he could not remain quiet in the chair. He started up and walked up and down the room.

'It was what I swore to Blackie; so I went and done it. But I ain't made no promise to you, Red, because I wanted to do by you more'n any promise could hold. What I aim for you is to make you into a fine gentleman. You hear me, boy?'

'I hear you,' said Red quietly, thoughtfully.

'Unless,' said Connell, 'you'd rather turn into a regular cow-puncher?'

'It's only about the name,' said Red slowly.

'Connell? Ain't that to your likin'? I tell you, Red, that you could go all through Ireland and never find a better name than Connell!'

'Sure,' said Red, full of embarrassment. 'It ain't that Connell ain't a good name.'

'What's workin' on you, then?'

'My father,' said the boy, 'was a tolerable proud man. He set a store by that name of Hardwick. You would of smiled to see how much store he put in it!'

'Hardwick,' said Connell, 'might be a good name. I got nothin' agin' it—except that it ain't

99

no better than Connell. Not a mite. You could hold up your head wearin' the name of Connell as high as anybody in the world, I aim to state!'

'Most like I could!'

'Well, then?'

'But if I was to think of pleasin' my father—I dunno that he'd take kind to me wearin' another name.'

Connell stopped in the midst of his pacing. Here was opposition of a sort which he could never have expected.

'Look here, Red,' he said kindly, 'I dunno that you understand. I've made Blackie my son. I've give him my name. He's got a right to inherit some of my money if I was to die tomorrow, say. Well, sir, that's just what I want to do with you. I want to make you my son, Red.

'Me and the old woman, we ain't had no luck in having children. And it's a lonely life livin' only by ourselves, we two old folks. Y'understand, Red? I've took in Blackie because of a promise that tied me down. Now I want to take you in, boy, because of the pure likin' for you. I want to make you as close to me as if you had my own blood in you, and how could I do all of those things unless that I had a chance to put my own name on you?'

Red nodded in the dusk. 'It's mighty fine,' he said softly. 'I take it mighty kind of you, Mr Connell. But—'

'But what?' snapped out the man. 'Are you

gunna think of reasons for why you shouldn't be made a rich man? Is that the way of it?'

'It's my father,' began Red faintly.

'Darn it, Red, ain't he dead?'

'I think of him tolerable often.'

'Would he be sorry to see you step into something fine and comfortable—with maybe a couple of *millions* to inherit one of these days?'

Red gasped as those immense figures struck across his mind.

'Millions!' he said.

'Ay,' said Connell proudly, 'because that's what it would be. You know what a million means?'

'It's a mighty pile!'

'Look here, Red, and I'm gunna make you *see* what it means. What does a puncher get a month?'

'Why, a real puncher, he gets a pile of money. Much as forty a month.'

'All clear money, ain't it?'

'Sure. He sleeps in his blankets. He gets his chuck, too. He gets that forty dollars all clear.'

'Well, sir, forty dollars ain't to be sneezed at. How would you like forty dollars a month all for yourself?'

Red gasped and then laughed. 'I ain't a plumb fool,' he said. 'Once I had three dollars and forty-five cents. I got that for workin' a month in the store.'

'H-m-m!' said the prospector. 'I understand.

101

You had that much all for yourself?'

'Yep. All of it.'

'Well, Red, suppose that a hundred men was workin' and all gettin' forty dollars a month. That'd be a pile of money every month, I guess?'

'Jiminy!' breathed Red. 'I guess that'd be about as much money as anybody could carry around!'

'It would be four thousand dollars a month, old son, and suppose that all of them men was to work right on through a year at forty dollars a month, at the end of the year that bunch of a hundred cow-punchers, supposin' that they was to save every nickel and not spend a cent, they'd have pretty close to a pile of fifty thousand dollars!

'Well, Red, I tell you that if all of them put their ten thousand dollars apiece into ranches, there would be a hundred pretty little ranches, wouldn't there?'

'Sure,' said Red.

Mr Connell growled in comfort. 'Young feller,' he said, 'lemme tell you that all of them hundred ranches wouldn't be worth no more than one million dollars, and that's just how much money a million dollars is!'

'Why, Mr Connell, have you really got that much?'

'I tell you, son, that I got more than that—a pile more! And if you was to be my boy and wear the name of Connell—you'd get what I got when I die. Blackie will get some. He'll get enough. I'll provide for him fine, because I promised that I would. But my heart is in you, Red. You done square by me.'

Then he heard the boy say slowly: 'Mr Connell, suppose that you was to have a son.'

'Which I ain't got none.'

'I'm just supposin'.'

'What good is there in supposin' what ain't? But go ahead. What are you drivin' toward?'

'Just this here idea. Suppose that you had a son that was wearin' your name. And suppose that pretty soon you died. Suppose that you didn't leave more'n one million to that boy. Then suppose that somebody come along that could build a whole house out of gold and put in diamond windows and everything just like in a fairy tale where they done everything by just making a wish. Well, sir, suppose this here feller come along and says to your boy: "You come along with me and be *my* boy! I got a thousand times as much money as your pa has got." I say, how would you feel in your grave, Mr Connell, if you was to know that your son give up your name and switched to the other feller's name?'

It had dawned upon Connell only gradually that the boy was working toward a definite refusal of his own great proffer. But he could not believe it until the last words were spoken, and still it seemed impossible.

'Look here,' he shouted, stamping on the

floor until the boards yielded and groaned beneath him, 'are you likenin' me to your father that was a beggar—me that am a millionaire?'

The shrill voice of the boy barked back at him instantly: 'You lie! He wasn't no beggar! He was a honest man—he wasn't no beggar! It's a lie! And if he was here, he'd lick you for sayin' that! If I could stand up, I'd show you what kind of a beggar he was!'

'You red-headed rat!' bellowed Connell. 'Maybe you're too good to be wearin' the name of Connell? Maybe you're too good? And maybe I'm too good to have you wear that name! Maybe I take back what I was offerin' you!'

'I don't want it!' shrilled the boy. 'I wouldn't have your name or your money! I don't want it!'

Mr Connell heaved up his great fist in the darkness. Then, upon a second thought, he wheeled and ran from the room.

CHAPTER THIRTEEN

RICA INTERFERES

Across the kitchen the big man lunged. He smote open the screen door with his clenched fist. He rushed out into the darkness. He did not pause until he reached the watering trough. There he stopped, dragging down great breaths to the bottom of his lungs, but still half stifled by his rage.

There is nothing so infuriating as that which we cannot understand. And yet, at the bottom of his heart he *did* vaguely understand and he did vaguely feel that Red was right. But that, for some reason, only increased his fury.

He had proffered millions to a penniless boy, and he had been refused! He wanted to break the youngster into a thousand bits.

The chickens, disturbed by some sudden night fear, broke into a clamor on their roosts. That harsh noise made half of the blind mist of fury clear from the brain of Connell. He was able to go back to the house, and when he entered the kitchen again, his face was iron.

Supper was ready. He washed his hands and face at the sink with a savage energy. Then he sat down without a word at his place. Neither did Mrs Connell speak for some time. She went about quietly ministering to his wants. She helped him enormously to liver and bacon. She poured his coffee, black as the waters of the river Styx. She heaped his plate with shining fried potatoes. She pushed toward him the plate piled with ample slices of bread. She edged toward him a dish of his favorite strawberry jam.

Then she said gently: 'The ingrate!'

Her husband flashed up a glance at her and

saw that her face was suffused with color, and that her eyes were dim with tears. He was greatly touched. He did not know that it was joy that brought the color to her face and the tears to her eyes. For she felt that what kept her at a distance from her husband, recently, was chiefly the two boys.

Blackie was sent away from the house. Now that she was delivered from his biting tongue and from his keen eyes which from the first day had been able to see through and through her, she had felt that she could make some progress toward winning back a measure of her old influence over Andy Connell. There was still Red, however, and he seemed unshakably intrenched in the heart of the miner. Now, however, she had a new hope.

'There ain't no makin' out a boy like that,' said Connell heavily. 'They're like mules.'

'Vicious, like mules,' agreed Mrs Connell. 'That boy is takin' advantage of your big heart and your good nature, Andy.'

'I would of made him rich!' snarled out Connell.

'He'd rather have his pride!' said the wife.

'I'll see him hang before I ever lift a hand for him again.'

She shook her head. 'You'll be over this here in a minute. You'll be fussin' around him again, then, and askin' his pardon for havin' hurt his feelin's—the brat!'

'Will I?' roared Connell. 'I'll go tell him

now—'

'Wait a minute, Andy.'

'I ain't gunna wait.'

'Make up your mind for yourself. There ain't no use tellin' him. He'd go around the country tellin' folks that you'd turned him out of your house—after him savin' your life.'

'He done that. God forgive me for forgettin' that!'

She saw that she had made a misstep, and she hastened to retrace her ground.

'He would of done it for a dog. He told me that himself.'

'Did he say that?'

'Sure he did! He laughs at you behind your back, Andy!'

'The young rat!'

She was silent, waiting, infinitely pleased with herself. She watched him stabbing at his food, sometimes pausing in angry thought:

'Why didn't you tell me these here things, Rica? Why didn't you tell 'em to me before?'

'Would you of believed me?'

He was silent again, and she went on, watching him carefully lest she should be tempted into saying too much: 'You see, Andy, you've pretty much forgot your wedded wife. You've held old scores agin' me. God knows that all I've done has always been for your own good. Ain't I been tryin' to make you happy? Ain't I been cookin' and slavin' for you all of these here years? Ain't I been keepin' a home together?'

Connell shifted in his chair.

'Then them two boys come home with you,' she went on. 'But it was me keepin' after you that made you start the plowin', wasn't it?'

'It sure was, Rica.'

'And wasn't it the plowin' that brung you to the gold?'

'Ay, Rica. That's true.'

'Then d'you owe that there money to Red, that was drivin' the plow, or to me, that started you to that work?'

He sighed and shook his head. 'That sounds all pretty fair to me.'

'Not that I'm claimin' nothin' for myself, Andy. Only it makes me sort of sad to see yourself actin' as though you owed everything to this here Red! This little ingrate!'

'Connell ain't a good-enough name for him!' growled out the prospector.

'It ain't?'

'Nope. He says that Hardwick is a name a pile above Connell. He wouldn't disgrace himself wearin' a name like Connell, not for a minute!'

'I'd teach him a lesson!' cried she.

'Oh, he'll cuss himself for what he's done to-day, before he gets to be a growed-up man!'

'I heard him talkin',' said she.

'You did?'

'I heard him damnin' you to your face!'

'I should of horsewhipped him—except that

108

he was so weak!'

'He wasn't too weak to laugh after you left the room.'

'What!'

'I said that he wasn't too weak to laugh!'

'At what?'

'Andy, at you, of course. I come to the door and asked what it was all about. He said that you was a fool! I told him not to make you mad, because you could do a mighty lot for him. He told me that he didn't care. He could get anything he wanted out of you, because you owed everything to him.'

These inventions she related with a sort of honest indignation and sorrow, as though she wondered that so much wickedness could exist as was lodged in the breast of Oliver Hardwick.

For a reward, she saw her husband forget his food and stare at her with the eyes of a bull, filled with a great wrath.

'Rica,' he said at last, 'it don't no ways look possible!'

'D'you think that I'd make it up?' she asked him, with the indignation of a natural liar. 'Oh, Andy, you're tryin' to break my heart! Why should I care what you do for Red? Ain't it him that stuck up for me when you tried to send me away that time when—'

'There ain't no use goin' back to that,' said Andrew Connell. 'I guess that I know you hate him, though. You want what I was tryin' to give him. But, by the heavens, now I'll give him nothin'!'

'Find him, Andy,' she whispered, 'and make him hear what you think of him—quick! Before that great soft booby heart of yours gets weak about him!'

'I'll find him,' he snarled out at her. 'Gimme a lamp, will you?'

She hastened back to the kitchen table and caught up the lamp. As a torch bearer to his anger she walked before him into the room.

'Now, Oliver Hardwick—' she began. But when she turned around and cast the light into every corner of the room, there was no sight of the boy.

'He's sneaked under the bed,' began the woman.

Here her husband caught her arm. He was staring down at the floor as if a black revelation were dawning upon his mind.

'He ain't under the bed,' he said. 'That ain't the way with a fighter like him. But maybe he's upstairs. Go look up there!'

He was so tense, and there was so much hidden in his low voice, that she gave him a single frightened glance and then hurried to obey him. He remained standing in the blackness of the room, the frown drawing tighter and tighter on his forehead.

Then her voice came from above: 'Why, Andy, he ain't up here! I have looked all over.'

She did not hear him reply, so she came down at once, busy with conjectures.

'He's gone off to the barn,' she declared. 'He likes the hosses a heap more than he cares for either of us. He's off in the barn, Andy!'

She saw her husband shaking his head. 'He ain't in the barn,' said he. 'But we'll go off and look there!'

They went out to the barn, their feet splashing through little puddles left by the recent rains, as noisy as voices in the sticky mud. So they came to the barn and looked inside. But when Mrs Connell raised the lantern for which she had exchanged the lamp in the house, its light glistened back to them only from the eyes of the horses, each with a raised head turned toward them. The boy was not there. Neither was he in the mow.

Andy Connell climbed down from the top of the hay and stood in that same black thought before his wife. Her fear was growing momently. She did not like silence in her husband. She could grapple with words and make a reply to them, but silence left her frightened and adrift.

'Rica,' he said at last, 'he went and left us!'

'Him?' she shrilled, quivering with excitement. 'Leave us and leave all the money that he hopes to get out of you? Even a boy couldn't be such a fool!'

'He's gone and left us.'

'But he could hardly walk, Andy!'

'He's gone. Rica, you been lyin' to me about what he said about me.'

111

She clamored at him, struck with terror: 'Andy, what're you sayin'?'

He insisted: 'He didn't call me no fool. He didn't laugh at me behind my back!'

She threw up both her hands. 'So help me—' she began.

But he struck both her hands down with an iron gesture. 'Woman,' said Andy Connell fiercely, 'what if God was to hear you?'

She grew white and her face wrinkled with a sudden dread; and the lie stood visibly printed on her features, a horrible thing to see. Connell turned his back on her and hurried out into the night.

The sky was cast about with clouds, low-sweeping, thick with deeper shadows in the blue-black sky. But in between were scatterings of stars, and against these the pines were stiff and black. Yet there was starlight enough to enable Connell to see the road, dotted with giant splotches of silver, where the water lay level in every depression, unriffled by a single wave, for the wind did not touch the earth. Only through the heavens an upper current swept the clouds grandly to the southwest.

And Connell, hurrying up the road, paused a moment to consider. He had started automatically toward the town, for that was the natural direction in which a man would travel. But Red Hardwick would not do what other boys would do. He went by opposites, and that opposite in this case was sure to take him up the road, where it went roughly through the hills and toward the storm-wrapped mountains, far away.

So Connell turned about and hastened away from the town of Jackson Corners, past his house again. It seemed to him a very ugly, small, insignificant shadow to have contained all the drama, all the great hopes, all the strange realizations, all the heart burnings, all the revelations of human nature which had been crowded inside its rude walls in the past few weeks.

He had looked upon it in the old days as the dominion of his wife over which she ruled with a scepter of iron, swaying him as she pleased. He looked upon it now as his own throne, which she shared only in so far as he chose to allow her. So much had the discovery of gold done for him.

Though money had gilded his life, it had touched the exterior only. All his heart was hollow with a sense of loss. What men and women said to him now could not be believed. They flattered him, as Jeffrey Morgan had flattered, as his wife flattered, as Blackie flattered. He knew it and he hated it, but he had not the skill to detect their impositions always. They were attempting to wheedle favors from him. Only Red was honest, and only with Red he could not get along. For Red told the truth, stood on his own feet, and looked the facts of his life squarely in the face.

Such were the thoughts of poor Connell as he struggled up the road, blundering through the mud, splashing through the water, filled with a burning shame until he was glad that the night would be there to cover his face in case he should find the boy. For how could he confront him?

Up a towering hillside, a tortuous and winding way, the road passed to a crest topped with trees. There he paused and scanned the road before him, and on the next hilltop he saw what he wanted—a small, slender form working over the summit against a group of stars.

And all the heart of Connell rose into his throat. There was pity, there was remorse, there was a giant's resolve to right at a stroke all of the wrongs which he had done to Red in his mind and in his acts. He shouted with all his force. At that the fugitive turned, and Connell waved. But apparently Red had no desire to be overtaken, for he turned once more and was instantly hidden behind the head of the hill.

It was incredible. And Connell, in a fresh burst of anguish, began to run down the slope. At the bottom of the dip, he tripped over some projecting stones, washed bare by the recent freshet, and landed heavily on his face in a flat pool. He rose, heavy with mud and drenched with water, his wind quite knocked out of him, but he scarcely heeded that. He did not pay it so much as the summary attention of a curse, but hurried on again with fumbling feet up the rise.

He gained the farther summit. Below him was a half-mile sweep of the road to the next hill, and beyond a shadow of a doubt Red could not have traveled so far in such a space of time.

So Connell hunted in a fury of anxiety. Now and again he stopped and shouted:

'Red! Oh, Red! Come back! We're all square. I was wrong! I was wrong, Red, d'you hear? Name of God, boy, I'm askin' you back! Red—'

And in the midst of one of these frantic appeals, he tripped over something soft at the corner of a great rock. And there lay Red, face down lest the whiteness of his skin should attract the searcher. Even now, though his ribs had felt the heavy toe of the boot of Connell, he did not stir, did not look up, as though he prayed that the man would go on and pay no heed to the thing over which he had tripped.

All of this was clear to Connell as he stood there, staring down at the boy. Then he picked him up, carefully.

'Red,' he said, 'I've come to tell you that I didn't mean what you heard me say about—'

Red shook himself free. 'I'm a sneak. I'm a liar. I'm tryin' to work you for your money. Why, darn your money! *I* don't want it. Find crooks to spend it on. Spend it on Blackie. I'll see you in purgatory before I'll take a penny out of you. I don't want it. Your money is dirt, d'you hear?'

Connell listened with a bowed head, his arms hanging helplessly at his sides.

'All right, Red,' he said, 'you can say all of that, and I got to stand here and take it and not say a word back to you, because you got a right to talk as much as you please. Red, I'm askin' you to forgive me!'

Apologies come hard, in the West. This one came stiffly from the lips of Connell, and Red was so astonished that half of his fury left him. He braced himself against the trunk of a small sappling.

'Partner,' said he to Connell, 'it looks like you and me couldn't get along. And since I'm to leave, I'll leave now. I ain't got the nerve to go back and face Mrs Connell ag'in.'

'I'll turn her out of the house,' said Connell. 'I'll send her to town, which is where she wants to go. But, Red, if you don't come back, I'll feel a skunk the rest of my days!'

'It ain't best, Mr Connell.'

'Look here, son, you're shakin' and can hardly stand.'

'I'll get on mighty well.'

'Red, I'm tellin' you man to man, so to speak, that I'm sick about this here thing. It was her tongue workin' on me. And you made me mad about the name.'

Red was silent and Connell hastened to add: 'But I've got over that. If you don't want to wear my name, keep your own. I ain't gunna pester you about adoptions. All I want to do is to give you a fair break. I want to give you a chance.'

'Thanks,' said Red stiffly. 'That's mighty fine. But I'd rather make my own chances. I'd rather not owe nothin' to nobody.'

Connell was baffled. He cast wildly about him. Here he was holding out a fortune in the hollow of his hand. Here was a child refusing it.

'It'll be a mighty sad day for you, Red,' he said, 'when Blackie comes home all dressed up fine, ridin' his fine hosses, and talkin' fine school talk as smooth as anything. And there you'll be punchin' cows and talkin' low, like me and the rest, and chewin' tobacco, and lookin' like a tramp.'

Red gasped. 'I dunno that I thought about Blackie.'

'He'd be layin' it over you pretty strong.'

'I can lick him every day of his life!'

'He'll be havin' fine boxin' teachers back there, and he'll be workin' hard to learn the tricks, and when he meets up with you when he comes back, he'll lick you easy, old son.'

There was a groan from Red.

'Come along home, Red. Here, gimme your arm. Lean on me. Dog-gone wet night, ain't it? Look where I fell down and got muddy from head to foot. Ha, ha, ha! Jiminy Red I thought I was never gunna find you.'

117

CHAPTER FOURTEEN

RED AT SCHOOL

So big Connell had come for Red and fairly forced him back to the house. And there Mrs Connell, when she heard their voices, came running out to meet them and took charge of him herself and bustled him into the house.

He fell into a happy, feverish sleep, waking now and again as though to listen to a storm— that storm was composed of the voices of the prospector and his wife talking heavily in the kitchen. He could hear snatches of the conversation now and again.

'Whatever I've said,' he heard Mrs Connell say once 'when I thought of the poor lad out in that rain and storm, it fair sickened me, Andy. God bless his brave heart.'

After that, he recovered by leaps and bounds, as the saying goes. The doctor was amazed by the daily progress. At the end of the week he was in town being fitted with clothes unbelievably good. And a week later still, he and Andy Connell sat in a room walled about with dusky books with a tall, thin, stern-looking man before them. It was Gregory Naseby, the headmaster of the Burton school.

'How far,' said Mr Naseby, 'have you gone in the public schools, Oliver?'

While Red blinked over that unfamiliar name, Connell put in kindly: 'He ain't had much of a chance, Mr Naseby. Take things by and large, he ain't put in much time in schools—'

'If you please,' said the icy Mr Naseby, 'let him answer for himself. Oliver, how far have you gone through the public schools?'

'Third grade,' said Oliver, and then remembering that he was twelve years old, he turned the brightest crimson.

But Mr Naseby did not seem at all surprised. He merely nodded.

'Third grade. Three grades better than nothing—a vast deal better than nothing. Do you like to study, Oliver?'

Red cast about him for help. He looked desperately at Connell. And the miner was nodding his head furiously. But the lie stuck in Red's throat.

'I hate it!' he groaned.

Something passed over the face of Mr Naseby. It could not have been a smile.

'Very well,' said he. 'You don't wish to study, but your good friend, Mr Connell, has persuaded you to come to school?'

Red explained savagely, seeing the despair in the face of Connell: 'He's givin' me the chance. I want to come bad enough. I'm mighty behind, but I can work.' He made a gesture with his muscular young arms. 'I'll work pretty hard! I'll work like the devil, Mr Naseby.'

Mr Naseby stirred in his chair.

'Put a half hitch on that sort of talk,' advised Connell hastily.

'I'm sorry,' said Red. 'It sort of popped out.'

'I think,' said Mr Naseby, 'that we may overlook this. You may go out into the yard, Oliver. You may see through the window the playground where they are at baseball now. I suppose that you play baseball, Oliver?'

'No,' said Red.

'You can learn, however.'

So Oliver Hardwick went out into the yard and left Connell alone with Mr Naseby.

'Now,' said Mr Naseby, 'there is a chance for you to tell me what you expect us to do for your boy.'

'He's kind of backward for his age,' explained Mr Connell, perspiring with embarrassment. 'He's been wastin' his time follerin' trails and shootin' guns and ridin' hosses.'

The headmaster smiled. 'Sometimes,' said he, 'I think that our boys might be far better off if they lived in that way past adolescence. We need eyes and ears. We lose them poring over our books. No, Mr Connell, there's plenty of material in Oliver, and it will be a pleasure to try to carve out a man. But the question is what sort of a man do you wish him to be?'

In one word the soul of Connell expressed itself: 'A gentleman, sir!'

It was the turn of Mr Naseby to blink.

'That,' he admitted, 'is a great deal. But we'll do our best. As for the terms,' he went on, scanning the rough boots of the Westerner casually, 'we will make them as moderate as possible. His allowance—'

'About the money,' said Connell, 'I've got a check here for ten thousand. I'm gunna leave it. You can give him as much money as you think will be good for him. You can fix him up with the sort of clothes that he needs. When that money is gone he'll have as much more as you say.'

The headmaster was busy readjusting himself to a new measure for Connell and the latter's protégé.

'He's got to get used to spending money,' went on Connell, 'because when I die he'll have a few millions to handle. About the sort of things that he'd ought to study, I dunno that I got book knowledge enough to talk about 'em. I leave that all in your hands, Mr Naseby.'

'This,' said the headmaster, 'is the sort of task that we are glad to undertake.'

So Connell left and Red remained in the Burton school. They said good-by at a silent dinner in the village.

'Are you gunna feel like a stranger, Red?' asked Connell.

'Maybe,' said Red, 'but I guess I won't mind that. What I'm gunna do is to try to turn myself into what a Hardwick had ought to be!'

He bit his lip, after that, realizing what a

double meaning the word might have for his friend, but Connell said nothing. Afterward, as he left, Connell said: 'Be square with everybody, Red, and they'll all end up by bein' square with you.'

So he departed, and Red went back to the school.

He found himself consigned to a dormitory in which every room was occupied by five boys, one of the older students, a sort of field captain for the rest, and four others of ages varying down to the youngest. He being that youngest was a sort of slave for the others until, a week after his arrival, he closed with a stalwart fourteen-year-old who was next him in age and engaged in a bitter battle. A table was wrecked and two chairs were broken by the impacts of their fiercely twisting, rolling bodies, but before ten minutes had passed the elder boy was flat on his back in a corner with a disfigured face turned up to the ceiling.

Then Red unbolted the door to those who were clamoring in the hall. He took his whipping without a murmur and then faced the lecture of the headmaster.

'I had to show 'em that I wasn't yaller,' explained Red, and that was all he had to say.

In the meantime, a special tutor was laboring to bring him up to the standard of his age. It was hard work for Red. His eyes, used to looking across the distances of the mountains, revolted at the nearness of the print and the dullness of the lessons, but his patience was that of an Indian upon the trail, and where there is patience and muscles in the brain, knowledge will come as a matter of course.

There were labors of another nature, too. He had to learn how to wear his clothes so that wrinkles did not crop up in them in five minutes. He had to learn to stand straight, to sit quiet, to talk softly, and, above all, to weed the slang from his speech. But just as a good horse responds to the whip, no matter what the load, so Red responded.

'Keep up this progress,' said the headmaster at the end of the term, 'and you'll be one of our best scholars in another three years.'

He carried that thought home with him for the summer where he found Connell waiting for him at the station.

'Blackie wanted to come, too,' said Connell. 'He's home a week before you. But I figgered that I'd better come alone.'

As he drove out on the familiar road he explained: 'Blackie has growed a lot, Red, and he's brung home a pair of boxing gloves.'

Then, with the old house in sight, he added: 'He's been workin' out with Si Jenkins, the blacksmith. Si used to want to be a prize fighter, and he dog-gone near come to be a good one till somebody busted his jaw for him.'

By this Red knew what lay in store for him, but only in part. When he saw Blackie, awe entered into his soul. That year of absence had tacked two and a half inches onto the height of Blackie, and he had filled out in proportion. He was thirteen, exactly the age of Red, but he looked a full two years older, and when he scanned the shorter and more clumsy form of Red at meeting, fire came into his glistening black eyes.

He found an opportunity during the supper to whisper: 'You and me are going to have it out, Red!'

But when they met behind the barn, after supper, Mr Connell himself came suddenly around the corner upon them.

'Boys,' said he, 'I've figgered this all out. You been workin' for a year to lick Red, Blackie, and right now you could do it. But wait for him to catch up and have a fair chance. I been talkin' it over with Jenkins. He's gunna give lessons to the two of you for a month. After that, you can have a go at each other, but not a minute before. Y'understand? Not a minute before, or I'll take it out of your hide, Blackie.'

Rage and disappointment gleamed in the eye of Blackie, but he saw too much resolution in the face of the prospector, and he dared not disobey.

And so, the next day, Jenkins came up to the house and Red began his first boxing lesson.

CHAPTER FIFTEEN

'THAT SHIFT!'

When Red first saw Si Jenkins, he decided that his eyes had fallen, at last upon the ugliest man in the world. And there could have been few who would have cared to dispute the prize with the blacksmith. In his youth he had been a man with no great pretentions to physical charm, and the fortunes of his physical life had not enhanced his beauty.

He went about his work in a businesslike way.

'First off,' said he, 'I'll put on the gloves with Blackie. You stand by and see how he works. You'll learn from him.'

Blackie, nothing loath to act as an example, pulled on the gloves. They were small, and the leather had been blackened with peculiarly ominous stains.

'I've taught my own kid how to box,' said Si. 'I got these here gloves for him to work out with. That's how I happen to have something to fit you. My kid learned to sling his mitts pretty fair. When you get good, I'll try you out agin' him. Now, Blackie, put up your props, and lemme see you lead a straight left.'

Blackie accordingly, stood on guard, with his weight evenly distributed on both feet, his

125

left hand extended, his head high. He feinted with his right for the body and then instantly stamped his left foot forward and darted his left fist at the face of his teacher.

'Look there!' said the instructor. 'He mighty near got me with that, even though I knowed what he was gunna try. That's what speed means! Look how he done it—stepped out with his left foot, put his body behind the punch, and had his right heel and leg and left shoulder all in a line. He's been havin' lessons before he ever come to me, I tell you. You can't teach nobody a straight left all in a minute.'

Thus he spoke, but at the same time, he seemed to be blocking the blow mechanically, without the slightest of mental efforts. The lesson proceeded, and Red, sitting on the top rail of the fence with his head sunk between his shoulders, watched with a glistening eye while Blackie demonstrated the straight left again, the right cross, rising on his toes, and, dipping his fist over the shoulder of his teacher, the right uppercut, the left swing for the body, an overhand smash with either hand while he ducked under a swinging attack. And in addition to this there was neat footwork which carried Blackie hither and yon across the ground with a gliding step.

When it was ended, Blackie took off the gloves, panting, and proffered them to Red.

'Now,' said Si Jenkins, standing up to the boy, 'what're you gunna figger on first.'

'I'm gunna figger,' said Red, 'on where I'm to hit you.'

The blacksmith shrugged his shoulders.

'You're wrong,' said he. 'You're gunna figger first on tryin' to keep from gettin' hit. Now block a straight left for the head. Hold your own right like this, see? Catch my glove on the inside of yours and brush it away—now!'

He struck as he spoke, his glove darting out like a snake's tongue, and Red strove to block. He had only one desire, and that was to do exactly as the instructor told him, but an instinct interfered. Instead of blocking, or even making an attempt to do so, his head rolled over on his shoulder—the gloved hand and the brawny forearm of the smith shot over his cheek, grazing his skin with the rough leather, and at the same time he stepped in and rapped his right hand against the ribs of Si Jenkins.

And the blacksmith grunted with the pain and the surprise. It was not all surprise, indeed. For between the two there was not such a vast difference in size. Si Jenkins had been a bantamweight in his ring days, and the years had hardened him rather than increased his bulk. And Red was a solid boy of thirteen, muscled from head to toe with smooth strength.

That punch, with the full sway of his body behind it as he stepped into Jenkins, sank well into the unprepared body of the ex-pugilist, and he grunted with the effect. His answer was as instinctive as the maneuver of Red. His right hand, carried high as he led with the left, now jerked across to the point of Red's jaw—a delicate little tap which traveled only a few inches, but it had the jerk of Jenkins' brawny shoulders behind it, and its effect was magical. It whirled Red around and pitched him to the ground on his face.

A swirl of crimson flashed before his eyes— crimson in black. It was part the stunning shock—it was part the flash of furious anger. He recoiled from the ground like a thrown rubber ball and leaped at Si Jenkins.

The blacksmith, in the meantime, stood back with an apologetic grin, but before he could speak, before he could explain, Red was at him. He pushed out both hands to stave off the onslaught.

'Hold on, kid—' he began, and then stabbed with a long straight left through the swirling arms and fists of Red. It was as inescapable as the lightning flash. It caught Red under the jaw and lifted him up and back. He staggered drunkenly a moment, then he lunged in again.

'Keep off, kid,' said Si, 'or I'll hurt you! Or d'you want me to stop, Connell?'

The prospector was watching with a lighted face. 'Handle him your own way,' said he. 'I ain't mixin' in with this here game. Don't let him muss you up!'

'Him?' said the blacksmith. 'He couldn't put

a glove on me. He tricked me, that first punch.'

As he spoke, he was picking off the punches of Red from all angles. A touch of his glove stopped a punch before it was well started, a raised elbow caught a swing and turned the hand of Red numb with pain, and the weaving forearms made an impenetrable wall against which Red battered in vain until he was gasping and snarling with rage.

'Stand back!' said Si. 'You little fool, are you fighting me?'

But there was no reason in Red. He was filled with one consuming passion, and that was to avenge the force in that first cruel blow which had knocked him down—a grown man—a trained fighter—to strike like that against a boy. It was not fair, and boys hate injustice.

Another sharp straight punch put him back on his heels. In the distance he heard Blackie crowing with glee. He heard old Connell saying: 'Red, you're playin' the fool. You'll never get at him!'

He heard them, but he did not see them. All that filled his eyes was the amused, keen face of the blacksmith—now transformed even in the midst of this petty battle! There was a flush in his swarthy cheeks, a glow in his small eyes. And as he moved about, his stepping was a poem of grace. At a drifting phantom, Red felt that he was striking. If he could land only once! If he could feel against his fist the sweet jar of bone grinding against bone.

He rushed once more, and the smiling blacksmith stood easily on guard, waiting. To plunge against those cunning hands was in vain. At the last instant he checked himself, as a bird checks itself in mid-air, and swoops toward the ground. So Red checked himself, striking out short with his left hand. Then, darting in again, he stepped out with his right foot and struck with his right hand. Just beneath the fluttering guard of Si Jenkins shot his fist, past that guard by magic—and the joy was already in his heart, and the hope!—under that guard and in, and then against his glove came the hard shock of the jaw bone sending a numb thrill up his entire arm.

His prayer had been granted—he had struck home! And with what effect! For Si Jenkins threw up his hands high and far apart and reeled back. Si Jenkins—the prize fighter! Si Jenkins, the man!

A madness of joy swept over the brain of Red. A sound that was a moan of delight quivered in his throat. He rushed in again, and again he saw Jenkins steady himself, but this time with blinking eyes of astonishment. And in the distance, now, there was the shout of dismay and wonder from Blackie, the shout of pleasure from the bewildered prospector.

'Soak him, Red!'

But as he rushed again at the retreating form of the smith, there was a change. Si Jenkins came forward with a puzzling little catch step, like a dancer. There was a look in his face which told Red that danger was ahead. In either threatening hand it seemed to lie. He would not attempt to parry—he would merely strike again—but just as Red poised himself for a third one of those peculiar attacks, the good left hand of Jenkins flicked out and it seemed to Red that a hammer stroke landed at the base of his skull. Darkness showered over him, and he dropped into an illimitable gulf of night.

He fell straight down, it seemed, for a long time, then steadied—then drew slowly back again. Before his eyes could see, his ears drank in sounds of which they made no meaning— the voice of Si Jenkins explaining to Connell:

'Where did he get it? Where did he learn it? Why, dog-gone me, I *had* to knock him stiff to keep from gettin' battered up myself! Connell, where did he get it?'

'God knows, not me. What was he doin' that bothered you, Si? He seemed to be hittin' you!'

'Seemed to be? Man, he was soakin' me with everything he had, and that's more'n any kid his age that ever I seen. If I'd been his own weight and age, he'd of knocked me kickin'! I tell you that! I'm sorry I had to hurt him, though. Blackie, fetch that water here.'

'Don't bother none,' said Connell. 'He's all made of India rubber. It ain't gunna hurt him none! He'll come up to his feet in a minute and want to start the fight all over again.'

'A game chicken—that's what he is!' declared the blacksmith. 'Fightin' stuff, that's what he's made of. I hit him hard enough to of knocked my boy Mike silly. This kid, he jumps up and comes back at me with a wild eye! Y'understand? He wanted to knock me stiff.'

He laughed, and broke off his laughter to gasp out: 'But where did he get it? He's been takin' lessons, Connell, and not tellin' you nothin' about it! What do you think of that?'

Here his full senses came back to Red, and he sat up with a sigh, blinked, and then started to his feet, snarling.

'Here, you young fool!' cried Si Jenkins. 'This ain't a fight. I hit you harder'n I meant to that first time. The second time, you *made* me hit you, and now, kid, come across with it. Tell me where you got it?'

Gradually it dawned upon Red that he was the center of admiring wonder, not of hostile ridicule. Yonder was Connell, his eyes shining in a telltale fashion. Yonder was Blackie, white and agape, as though he had just looked upon the end of the world.

'Where I got what?' asked Red, puckering his brow.

'Come on,' cajoled Si Jenkins. 'Lemme have it. Who's been teachin' you to box?'

'Nobody,' said Red frankly.

Si Jenkins merely shook his head. 'Maybe you just learned nacheral how to duck a fast straight left and counter with your right. Eh?'

'I dunno what you mean,' said Red, staring.

'Come on,' said Jenkins impatiently. 'That shift, young son. Where'd you learn that shift—and doggone my eyes if it ain't a beauty!'

'Shift?' said Red, quite at sea. 'I dunno what a shift is, Mr Jenkins!'

The blacksmith studied him through a somber moment.

'Connell,' he said, staring at Red and not looking at the prospector as he spoke, 'lend me this here kid for a couple of hours. And let me do what I want with him.'

'He's yours!' said Connell.

'Now,' said the blacksmith, 'you come along with me. I'm gunna find out.'

CHAPTER SIXTEEN

HOPES FOR RED

Red was ushered into the buggy of Si Jenkins and they straightway drove for the town. It was a silent ride. All that Si Jenkins could think of was a remark or two about the weather, and a few questions about Red's school, which Red himself answered with monosyllables. For one thing, his head was clearing only gradually and the weight was lifting from his brain.

They reached the town. They wound

133

through the dusty main street. They came at last in front of Jenkins' blacksmith shop where his partner was busily at work. At the rack they hitched the horse and started back through the shop.

'Hey, Si,' said his partner, 'old man Thomas wants to know when does he get them shares that you was to sharpen when—'

'Darn old man Thomas,' said the ex-fighter. 'I'm busy!'

Right in through the shop they went and into the back yard of the Jenkins' house which lay behind the shop itself. There Jenkins raised his voice:

'Mike! Oh, Mike! Roll out here and lemme have a look at you, kid!'

Presently the back door of the house slammed and Mike appeared upon the back porch, sleepily rubbing his eyes. He was a stalwart of fifteen, was Mike, built after the broad-shouldered type of his father, but upon a much larger scale. He was solid as a rock.

'Come down here,' said his father, and when he came, he tossed a pair of the boxing gloves to the boy. The other pair he laced over the hands of Red.

'Now, kids,' said he, drawing a five-dollar gold piece from his pocket, 'this here is for the one of you that wins this here scrap. Y'understand?'

He stepped back.

Red regarded his opponent with some

134

dismay, for the repute of Mike had gone forth on wings before him. He was a boy of might and a hero of many and many a battle. In either hand he bore a lightning flash, and in his mind was the cunning imbibed from the long lessons which his father had lavished during years upon him.

He was not tall, was Mike, but yet he was a shade above Red, and in bulk he was much greater, to say nothing of the two precious, seasoning years which brought him almost to the verge of manhood, while Red was still a full-fledged boy. Now Mike looked over his antagonist with the consciousness of superior power in his eye.

'What you got agin' Red, dad?' he asked. 'Why d'you want him beat up?'

Thus was the match touched to the tinder of Red's uneven disposition.

'You flat-faced yap,' said Red impolitely, 'I'll smash you for that.'

'Why, you runt!' exclaimed Mike, 'I'll knock your head off for you.'

And he swung his right hand up in a long-range uppercut, rising on his toes to give venom to the punch. Had it landed, the battle would have been ended, perhaps, before it well began, but an instinctive shrinking back caused the blow to miss by a fraction of an inch. And Red, in turn, slammed his fist straight at the face of the blacksmith's son. That blow was caught in a soft pocket—the inside of the gloved palm of Mike. Another tremendous swing sang through the air as Mike ducked under it.

'Why, dad,' said Mike, 'this kid don't know nothin'.'

Straightening, he drove both hands against the head of Red and sent him staggering back. Si Jenkins was in a black study. One might have thought that he was very ill pleased by the success of his own son in this battle.

'It looks queer,' he admitted.

'He can't even hit straight,' said Mike, blocking a swing with careless ease. 'I could knock his head off any time.'

'Go ahead and try it, then,' said Jenkins. 'I *can't* be wrong. If he ain't been taught, I'm a fool—I ain't got no eyes.'

'All right,' said Mike, 'here goes,' and he attacked like a whirlwind.

There were cruel handicaps for Red to stand against in the nature of age, weight, and above all the wisdom which he soon found to reside in the trained hands of Mike. The punches of the blacksmith's boy traveled as straight as rifle bullets. One may ward a swing as the fencer easily turns a broad-sword cut.

But a straight punch is like the sinister, darting point of a rapier. Through the guard of Red poured those wicked punches like water raining through a sieve, and every punch carried a sting. His nose was numb, his right eye shooting with pain, his ribs well thumped, and all of this in half a minute. He reeled before the assault.

'Here's the finish!' cried Mike, growing savage as with the taste of blood and victory, and he stepped close and drove with the full force of his good right fist.

Blocking would not do to stop that punch; at least, the simple blocking which Red understood would not. He did what he had done when the prize fighter drove for his face, he dropped his head upon one shoulder, let the punch shoot past, and then hammered his right into the pit of Mike's stomach.

What is so disheartening as a stomach punch? It dissolves the happy mist of victory at a touch. It puts in the very soul of a fighter a strange disgust for life. So it was with Mike. He doubled up and went reeling back.

'I told you!' cried the smith, as though delighted, 'When you think that you got him, he's got you. Look out now, Mike!'

For as Mike recovered his wind and straightened, Red charged him.

'I'll *kill* him,' panted Mike, and poised himself to meet the shock—poised himself with a light in his eyes and his jaw set. And well did Red know, by the look in that face, that if this attack failed, he, Red, would never endure to deliver another rush. And he remembered, then, this singular trick which had served him so well against the father of Mike.

He paused in the midst of the rush, like a

syncopation in music, or a two-step in the flow of the dance. He tried it again. Not so swiftly or so surely as against the father, for that had been a subconscious effort, so to speak, and this was done with forethought.

But nevertheless it succeeded. He paused, feinted with his right hand, then pivoted on the right foot and smote with his left as his body whirled in. All the weight of that body was in the blow, and all the speed of the whirl, and all the leaning impetus of the lunge forward. He saw his fist flash over the shoulder of Mike. He felt it jar home against the base of the jaw, but far different was the effect of the blow upon a boy from that which it had had upon the matured strength of a man.

Even Si Jenkins had been staggered, but his son, poor Mike, was hit completely off his feet. He crashed upon his face, swerving in his fall, and lay there on the grass with his arms cast out wide. His father, with a muttered exclamation, ran in and lifted the prostrate figure.

The head of Mike lolled back on his shoulders.

'Where am I?' groaned Mike. 'Somethin' landed on me from up top.'

'A fist,' said his father grimly. 'You've got what you've give other boys. Want to try a go at him again?'

'Yes!' yelled Mike. 'I'll kill him, this time. Lemme at him, dad!'

Si Jenkins caught his coat with a restraining

138

force. 'That sounds fine,' said he. 'But I ain't anxious to have your face spoiled for you. You ain't got no good looks to spare. This kid'll smash you to bits, Mike. He's got a man's punch, I'd say.'

He added: 'Get along to the house. You ain't won the money, but you ain't disgraced. *No* kid could lick Red the way he hits.'

So Mike went with fumbling feet toward the house, and the blacksmith turned on Red.

'Now, son,' said he, 'tell me the whole of it. Who taught you?'

'Mr Jenkins, if I knowed what you meant, I'd tell you. But I ain't had no teachin'. That duckin'—well, when I seen you hittin' so hard and so fast, I sort of *had* to do that, instead of what you was tellin' me.'

'Let that go. But the shift—the shift! What about that? What taught you to stop as fast as that in the middle of a rush and then shift around and hit with the other hand—hit fast as a flash!'

'Oh,' said Red, 'I dunno. I stumbled into that.'

'Stumbled, the devil!' exclaimed the blacksmith. 'And yet—dog-gone me if you didn't look pretty raw agin' Mike. He was playin' with you till you uncorked a ton of dynamite and blowed him up. It'll do him good. It'll make him stop playing the bully. It'll give him some sense and make him stop wantin' to be a prize fighter when he grows up.

'But, Red, lemme tell you this here—they's one punch that's harder than all the rest and the worst to get home, and that's the shift. Most gents, even prize fighters, can't work it. It means that your feet and your hands and your body has got to be workin' together, or else it won't work. And you, Red—you do it perfect, pretty near.'

This eulogy and analysis he pronounced in a voice of the greatest gravity.

He added: 'I'm gunna teach you, Red, to be what they ain't so many of in the world—a finisher.'

That was the end of the lesson for this day. He took Red back to the Connell house and there he left him, but before he left he sought out Blackie.

'Blackie,' said he, 'I got sort of an idea what you want to do, but don't fool yourself none. This here Red is poison for you. Understand? He's poison. Keep away from him.'

CHAPTER SEVENTEEN

A NEWCOMER

This was all in the beginning. But when Mr Jenkins was convinced that Red had indeed received no instruction whatever in the gentle art of self-defense—that his attainments were

140

all those of one self-taught—his wonder knew no bounds.

He admitted that this explained a certain recklessness, a certain inability to block with skill, but still there were features which he could not have expected, he declared, in any novice. He could not have expected a certain weaving style of attack. He could not, above all, have expected a perfect shift.

Afterward he explained what that shift meant, and how it was the hardest blow which could be struck, but rarely used because most men are so hopelessly clumsy in the execution of it.

'Some hosses pace; some trot; a shift is like a pace. Most hosses are trotters and never could learn to pace except mighty poor. Most gents can never learn to shift fast enough to fool anything bigger than a kid. But you got a shift as plumb nachcral as eatin' bread and jam. I can see now that even all the teachin' in the world never could of done that for you. It's got to be born in a gent.

'If you was to go ahead and take care of yourself, you might have the making of a champeen yourself, Red. You got the build. You grow to a heavyweight, too. Champeen of the world, Red, think of that.'

All of this was talk which could not fail to sink deep into the heart of Oliver Hardwick, and it bore fruit later on in his strange life. But, in the meantime, he was interested in only one great thing, and that was the complete destruction of Blackie.

'I want to stand up to Blackie,' he said. 'D'you think that I could?'

'You?' said the blacksmith. 'Well, Blackie has got a fine fighting heart, and he's fast, and he hits hard for a boy, but considerin' how much more my boy Mike knows about the game, and how much bigger and older he is, I guess that Mike would cut Blackie to pieces inside of three minutes, and you know for yourself what you done to Mike. Well, I s'pose that Blackie would stand up to you till you tried your first shift, and then he'd go down for keeps.'

Thus was the great victory stolen from Red. With all his heart he wanted to close again with Blackie and have out the fight with him, but now that he had stumbled upon this great bonanza of power, it would be like pitting a rich man against a beggar in finance. Out of his excess of might, how could he stoop to engage in battle with an inferior, a mere normal boy, like Blackie?

Yet simply because he had a certain natural ability, Mr Jenkins was by no means willing that Red should stop work.

'All you got is the beginnin' of something. No matter how hard or how *queer* a gent can hit, they's always the chance that he'll run into one of them fast, fancy boxers that keep dancin'. Well, Red, you could never be a dancer, because you like to root your feet into the ground and punch with all your might. But you can learn enough to take care of yourself while they're peckin' away at long range, and you could get fast enough to catch one of them dancers—and then good night to him.

'But right now is when you got to learn. What you learn about boxin' before you're fifteen sticks in your head the rest of your life. What you learn afterward, you always got to keep practicing or else you'll forget it. That's the trouble with me. I started in to learn too late. I always had to keep on practicin'. I never had no nacheral talent that was brung out young.'

Thus seriously did Si Jenkins talk. And Red, delighted by this great new thing at which he excelled, took the words of the blacksmith as gospel. Every day he had to sit at his book until the mid-afternoon, from the early morning, for he was desperately eager to make up the wasted years of his life in which there had been no study.

But when the mid-afternoon came, he swung onto the back of a horse and dashed for town, and in the cool of the evening he stood up to the blacksmith.

So he worked all summer, but not without a new interest coming in before the end, for after Blackie heard about the dreadful prowess of Red, and that natural aptitude in fisticuffs which he for his part could not hope to rival, he

143

began to lose all interest in the boxing game. Instead, he induced Mr Connell to buy him a small six-shooter, and a quantity of ammunition. With this he practiced day after day and day after day.

And when Red mentioned it one day and inquired why Blackie had given up his glove work—inquired with a certain sinister interest, Blackie replied with a sort of lofty calmness: 'Why, boxing is for ruffians. No gentleman is very much interested in it.'

It was a facer to Red over which he pondered seriously. Then he went to Connell.

'I'd like to have a revolver,' said Red.

The prospector grinned. 'I knowed that that was comin',' said he, 'but it won't do. It's too late this summer to start. Next summer you can shoot your head off if you want to. But wait till then. Ain't you ever handled a gun, Red?'

'When I was floatin' around,' said Red, 'I always had one along sort of for company.'

'H'm!' said the prospector. 'Maybe guns'll come nacheral to you like boxin', Red?'

Guns and boxing were not the only interest, however, for there was still another item to enter before the summer was over. A month before their time came for returning to their schools, the whole neighborhood was immensely excited by the tidings that they were to have a new member of the community in the person of a Mr Chalmer Greenough who had decided to come West for the purpose of establishing himself on a great farm where he could be surrounded by dogs and horses to his heart's content and where his children could be raised under an open sky.

Certainly he began to operate on a large scale. The news rushed suddenly to the general merchandise store in Jackson Corners and from the store veranda shot out again by a hundred human wires through all the country around—that Chalmer Greenough had bought the entire lower valley of Yates Creek. The news of the purchasing of the valley was a thunderstroke.

'What,' said Andy Connell, 'could he want with that?'

In the meantime, there were more and stirring events in Yates Valley. For all at once a whole army of workmen ascended to the lower edge of the upper valley—that is to say, to the mouth of the cañon. On those rock walls they swarmed. They began drilling and blasting. They broke enough ground to have made a mine and a good-sized one, and the entire country-side marveled at this insane waste of money.

'He's lookin' for gold!' said Connell. 'Lookin' for gold there! My heavens, there ain't a sign of color closer'n five miles of him, not unless it is right here on the Connell ranch.'

So said Connell, and there could be no doubt that he was right. What else could explain the strange proceeding and the blasting at the cliffs? But presently vast quantities of cement were shipped to the mouth of the cañon—part of it to the cañon, and part to a place farther down the valley, among hills overlooking the river. On a broad-topped hill other gangs had ripped away the surface dirt and gone down to the bed rock. Upon this rock lines of concrete wall were now erected. On and on it stretched, and furious rumor rushed wildly about the countryside.

'It ain't a house that he's gunna build. He's gunna build a whole town,' said Connell, who spent much of his leisure examining the progress of the idiots in Yates Valley.

'You take an Easterner and put him out West,' said Connell on another occasion, 'and you're pretty sure to have a darned queer sort of a man!'

Then the truth came with a stunning force. The mouth of the cañon was to be blocked with a great dam for which this was merely the preparatory work! The wonder of it lasted a fortnight and more. Then they saw the great foundations rise, incredibly thick; huge cranes swinging boulders of a giant size, and the swarming people dwindle to ants compared with the bulk of this thing they were constructing with borrowed arms and hands of steel and muscles of steam.

What a symbol of power, of limitless, exhaustless power those walls of the great house seemed to Red Hardwick as he strolled around them, gaping at the workmen. How cavernous deep were the excavations for the cellars—not a single cellar, but two stories deep, hollowed into the rock! The house was like a miracle performed in the desert; the dam was a veritable prodigy.

Finally, then, the great man himself came!

CHAPTER EIGHTEEN

BLACKIE'S GLORY

It happened in the following manner: Andy Connell had driven to Jackson Corners with Blackie and Red to spend Saturday afternoon. It was a regular ceremony. Not that there was a peculiar attraction about the little town on that day of the week, but every one who could, wandered into the place and there they sat about playing card games, or chatting on the capacious veranda of the hotel.

On this day, the three had barely reached the hotel, and Red was about to start off to find his friend and tutor, Si Jenkins, when a murmur ran down the street, like the first sighing breath of the wind which announces the coming of the storm. The murmur grew. It called all heads toward the eastern end of the street; it grew into a form and then: 'It's Mr Greenough and his two kids, Hugh and Beatrice.'

He had two children then, thought Red. How perfect was the position and the happiness of this man of men. He conjured up a vision of Mr Greenough, tall, stately, handsome, with a deep, quiet voice, and a steady, keen eye—a gray eye, penetrating, quiet, the sign of strength. Here he came, wrapped in the romance of the millions which with his own wits he had torn from the world. And his two children beside him.

'A right smart pair of kids,' said a tall Missourian. 'I heard ma tell about 'em. She seen 'em both yesterday.'

Then they appeared around the next corner of the winding street, the three all mounted, and mounted each exactly in propriety. There was the man on a strongly built charger, a big bay, and the boy on a lightweight racer, walking daintily like a tiptoe dancer, and the girl, last of all, on a hackney-built mare. A fortune, perhaps, for the price of these animals alone. Ah, money was no object to this Crœsus.

Now they were closer, and one could make out the features of the riders, but what a disappointment to Red when he saw the face of the great man clearly. Gone was the vision of handsome dignity, and in its place there remained a grossly built man with a hawk nose and a red, fat face, and thick wide shoulders, and a muscular air of self-content.

As for the boy, he was a golden-haired youngster of perhaps fourteen—the metal glint

148

of that hair shone in the slant sunshine beneath the brim of his derby. He had a pale, delicate, beautiful face, certainly never inherited from his father, and he managed his horse with a graceful ease. That fine-limbed thoroughbred moved on a loose rein, playing with its bits, turning its head here and there to look where it would, but patently at the disposal of its young master, perfectly in tune with him. Red had never before seen such horses, ridden with English pads; but he knew perfect horsemanship when he saw it.

His heart went out in admiration to the rider, in spite of the haughty expression of the boy's face. As for the girl, she rode more as her father did, with a stiff rein; and yet her mare seemed to love that control, or to mock it. For the chestnut came on eagerly, its ears pricking back and forth. She was unlike the other two, this girl. She had her father's force, her father's dark skin and black hair, but she had a graceful beauty like her brother's—with more of spirit in it. She was twelve, perhaps, just between childhood and womanhood, with some of the charm of both ages. She came upon the mind of Red like a fragrance upon the senses—a fragrance blown from a strange shore where ships have never touched.

He looked aside. There was Blackie standing stiff, transfixed. And Red was amazed. He had felt that there was nothing in the world which could make Blackie forget himself, really. He

149

had thought that there was nothing in the world which could move the boy except his own narrow self-interest. But this was a revelation. There was marvel and worship in the face of the boy. There was simplicity; there was sorrow. For the first time in his life, Red felt that it might be possible to find a friend in his ancient foe.

Then Joe Hooker's new pinto gelding, a beautiful and savage little demon lately off the range, and now tethered farthest down the hitching rack before the hotel, flung himself back and snapped short the reins by which he was held.

What impelled him no one could tell, unless it were the bubbling devil in his nature. But, throwing himself back in this fashion, he came just in front of the mare which the girl was riding and promptly proceeded to clear his way behind by lashing out with his heels.

Luckily they were unshod, but the spat of the bare hoof on the flank of the mare was like the clapping of hands together.

Red saw the mare rear with a squeal of pain, and saw the girl, with a frightened cry, cling suddenly around the neck of her mount.

He waited to see no more. That was enough. He leaped from the veranda and made for the scene. Other people were striving to get there also, but they took the more roundabout way. Red went straight as a homing pigeon. That his path had to be under horses did not disturb

150

him. He dived under a pair of them, missing their stamping hoofs by a fraction, and rolled to his feet beyond. There was the pinto, ears back, heels working, whirling here and there to get in a finishing drive at the mare. And yonder was the mare, in a fighting frenzy also, doing her best to gain revenge, while her mistress clung to the mane and screamed for help.

Red saw his grip and like a bulldog froze to it. He caught the bridle on either side of the bits, diving for it as a dog dives at another. His grip he made good, and then hung with all his weight.

Even a range mustang, toughened by range weather and range fights, will not care to perform while a sturdy thirteen-year-old is dangling from his head. The pinto hastily made off from the little hackney mare and presently, as though by present good behavior to escape from punishment for past mistakes, stood calmly, head down, beside the hitching rack, surrendering his head to Red and for all the world like a sleepy horse which had drowsed in the sun all the afternoon.

Then Red could look to see what else was happening. And he saw a thing that brought his heart into his mouth. For yonder was his companion, his somber rival, Blackie and none other, holding the hackney by the bits just as he was holding the pinto. Blackie, then, had flown to the scene as he himself had done. It was staggering to Red. He knew that Blackie was

151

brave enough, but always for himself first, and for no other. Here he had taken a chance with that rearing, plunging, fight-maddened mare, and for the sake of another, a stranger.

Mr Greenough, swinging his horse beside the mare dexterously, had swept Beatrice from the saddle. Now he sprang to the ground with her. Red expected to see her fainting in the arms of her father. There was not a bit of it. She was merely flushed, and her eyes were shining.

'I was silly to make so much noise,' Red heard her say. 'But I lost my head. I'm sorry, daddy.'

'Heaven bless my soul!' said Greenough. 'It came on us with such a jump—where the devil is that pinto now? No wonder you lost your head. However, I would have expected better of you. You may thank this youngster, Be. He caught Bunting just as she was about to slip you over her rump and drop you into the dust where the pair of the demons could have stamped your life out. You may thank this lad. He came in like a flash. Very brave! What's your name, boy?'

'Lewis Jason—' said Blackie, and added with a little start: 'Connell—Connell!'

'That's three names,' said the rich man, grinning. 'All right, young Mr Connell, you can have six names if you choose, and I'd remember them all. Beatrice, you owe a safe hide to this youngster.'

She was standing before Blackie—a slender

girl, but already with an air, and all her loveliness multiplied with excitement. To be where Blackie stood, Red felt that he would have given his life—without a thought. And now she was taking his hand. She was smiling into his face.

She spoke like a boy, in a strong, clear voice, and with a boy's words.

'That was a bully thing to do,' said she. 'It would have been a mess except for you.'

But he could never have answered—not in a thousand lives—as Blackie answered.

'There were a dozen others ready,' said he. 'I was only lucky enough to be first, Miss Greenough.'

That year at school had not been wasted on Blackie. Here he was with his newly learned manners on tap, and his newly pruned vocabulary. And how calm he was, how perfectly at ease as he stood before her and smiled in answer to her smile.

Now Greenough himself had Blackie by the hand. 'Young Mr Connell,' said he, 'you're a trump. The ace of trumps. Have you a father hereabouts? I have a word or two to speak to him.'

They were going back toward the hotel veranda, the crowd of men who had arrived too late to take a share in the rescue—to their infinite humiliation—following around them. And then Red heard a voice at his ear.

'Looks like Blackie gets all the glory, Red.

But I guess some of us know who done the *real* work.'

And there was tall Joe Hooker standing beside him, Joe Hooker the bronc peeler, the gun fighter, the chosen reckless spirit of the entire community, the bad example which was held up to frighten unruly youths. He was a man to conjure by. And this word of praise from him came like a blessing upon the mind of Red.

'I'm mighty glad I got the pinto,' said Red. 'He might of cut loose and run for it.'

'Darn his ornery hide,' said the slow voice of Joe Hooker. 'I reckon I'd never seen him ag'in. It was back to the range for him, says I to myself when I seen him bust the reins. I was a fool to tie him up like that.'

He reached into his pocket, and then changed his mind. He laid a hand on the shoulder of Red and looked down into his face with steady blue eyes, pale blue eyes, like the eyes of Red himself, fearless, bold, eager eyes. And Red could feel that glance, so it seemed to him, to the very core of his soul.

'I seen it all,' said Joe Hooker. 'I ain't forgettin'. I'd like pretty well to give you something to remember me by, Red. But I'll put it this way. When you need a friend, one of these days, you come and tell me what sort of a corner you want.'

All else was blotted from the brain of Red. Here was a golden opportunity thrust upon

154

him.

'D'you mean that, Mr Hooker?' he asked.

'I reckon I do, son.'

'You can do more for me than any other gent on the range.'

'Turn loose and talk, kid,' said the puncher.

'You can teach me to shoot.'

A shadow passed over the face of the tall man. 'Red,' he said, 'I've give you my promise and I'll stick to it. But think it over. There ain't anything in the world that I wouldn't rather do than that.'

'Next summer,' pleaded Red, 'when I get back from school—'

'You're set,' grunted Joe Hooker. 'Well, we'll leave it like that for the present.' And he turned short upon his heel.

CHAPTER NINETEEN

A SINISTER IDEA

Shame was raging in the blood of Blackie as he went toward the veranda of the hotel with his millionaire companion, and with Hugh Greenough and Beatrice Greenough following. That they should meet Connell as his bona fide father was too much, and he could not help saying, as he went forward: 'Mr Connell is not my real father, Mr Greenough.

155

He adopted me. My real name is Lewis Jason.'

Mr Greenough cast a sharp glance at the crimsoned face of the boy—a glance so sharp that something withered in Blackie. He felt as if he had been probed to the quick.

'All right,' said Greenough. 'Blood is one thing—names are another.'

They came to the veranda. And there was Andy Connell standing before them, rather proud of Blackie for distinguishing himself in this fashion, and for bringing such a focus of public attention upon himself and his family, but desperately determined to show not a whit of that pride.

Indeed, he was not a particularly dignified figure as he stood there. The clothes which had been new and good when he first returned after striking gold, had been so carelessly and so roughly used that the trousers were shapeless bags, and his coat a much-spotted wreck of its former glory. He had an ancient felt hat upon his head, a hat which had once been black but which time and the strong sunshine had turned to a decided green tint. His shirt had been blue—it was sun faded and washed to a dirty gray, and now it was opened at the throat, with the necktie sadly askew, so that Mr Connell could enjoy more air on this hot day.

To complete the picture he wore upon his feet a comfortable but enormous pair of old boots which had protected him from the rocks on many a journey through the highlands, and upon which the stones had carved their million initials busily.

This was the man to whom Blackie found himself introducing new acquaintances far above the finest flights of his fancy. And he gritted his teeth in despair and covertly watched the faces of the three. However, no matter what they might have thought, they were too perfectly schooled to betray the slightest trace of scorn. Only in the eye of Mr Greenough was there the faintest twinkle of amusement, but that was perceptible only to a witness as keen as the lynx-eyed Blackie. All three shook hands formally with Mr Connell. And he, with a determined effort, made himself perfectly at ease even with such dignified company.

'Glad to meet you, Mr Greenough,' he said. 'We been havin' a lot of talk about you in these parts. We been seein' your work every day, mostly, and we been hearin' it, too. Dog-gone me if I can't hear that work clean over to my place.'

He laughed heartily at this feeble jest and went on: 'Well, young feller'—this was to Hugh—'I hope you'll take a likin' to this part of the country. It'll put beef on your bones, I tell you. But your girl here, Mr Greenough, I reckon that she's pretty well fleshed up already.'

Blackie writhed in a mute agony, and still his foster father was speaking. Would he never

157

have done?

'While you're meeting the family,' said he, 'they's one more nigh at hand, I guess. Hey, Red!'

His voice rolled in thunder down the street, and the crowd, giving way a little, revealed Red in the act of slipping around the corner of the hotel. But Connell saw him and hailed him: 'Red! Hey, Red! Don't go sneakin' off. Got some friends here that are hankerin' to meet you.'

Red, hailed in this fashion, paused for a moment, as though he still was turning over the possibility of flight in his mind, but he had to come forward and be the subject of the proud speech of Connell.

'Here's Red—here's my other boy. Oliver Hardwick is his real name, but he's as much mine as Blackie is, I s'pose. You've took a shine to Blackie because he stepped out and had a chance to turn a hand for you. Well, sir, I'm tellin' you that he ain't no whit better'n Red. There was Red divin' for the head of Joe Hooker's pinto, and holdin' him just as well as Blackie held your mare, young lady.'

The black eyes of Beatrice fixed upon Red, and his own eyes sank to the floor, as though a weight pulled them down. With all his heart he wanted to be at ease, as Blackie had been. But in spite of himself, the red was mounting to his face. And the knowledge that his flush was seen completed his rout.

158

In the meantime, some acknowledgment had to be made of his services, so strongly forced upon the attention of the Greenough family.

'I'm sure,' said Beatrice coldly, 'that I am very greatly obliged.'

And: 'A fine lad, I see,' said Mr Greenough, and yawned a little.

'About my young friend, here,' he went on, as Red withdrew with all possible speed, 'I can't help telling you that I've taken a great fancy to him. I'd like to have him drop over and spend a few days with us while we're traveling around the valley—the Yates Valley you know. No doubt he knows the country very well and could point out some of the sights to us. Could you spare him to us, Mr Connell?'

The heart of Blackie leaped. 'Of course!' cried he. 'That would be mighty nice, Mr Greenough.'

'All mighty fine,' said Connell. 'But Blackie is pretty nigh to the time when he goes back to school. He'll have to be grindin' away at his books to get ready for studyin' in real earnest. Mighty kind of you, Mr Greenough. But I'll have to keep him at home.'

'The devil!' murmured Mr Greenough, and favored the old prospector with another of his searching glances. 'Very well, Lewis. I'll make a point of seeing you again before you leave. Beatrice—Hugh—we'll ride on. Good-by, sir. Good-by, Lewis.'

159

He was gone, and Blackie remained behind, stunned. He watched them trail off up the street; then the voice of Connell, turned suddenly harsh, roused him.

'Blackie, I'm gunna have a word with you. Come off here with me.'

They strolled around the corner of the hotel, Blackie in the depths of despair.

'You'll be wonderin',' said the prospector, 'why I didn't let you go. Lemme tell you that it was because I seen the look in your eye. Fine folks might put queer ideas into your head, Blackie. You got some already. And the best thing for you is to live quiet and common with the rest of us.'

To Blackie it seemed such an outrage that he could not make a reply for a moment; and when one did come to his lips, he decided to restrain it. He waited until they had left the town and returned to the Connell house before he opened his heart, and then he spoke in all the bitterness of his grief, the moment he could be alone with Mrs Connell. They had only one thing in common, and that was an intense dislike of Andy Connell. But this was enough to bring them close.

Mrs Connell heard the boy with solemn attention. 'It's jealousy, Blackie,' said she. 'All that Andy cares about is Red. You and me, what are we to him? You gettin' the promise out of him is all that made him adopt you. Sure it wasn't no likin' he had for you. And what does he want of me? Just to torture me by keepin' me here drudgin' on this place when I might be livin' like a lady off a mite of the money that he's puttin' away—the miser!'

Thoughts were born quickly in the agile brain of Blackie. One came there now, and he brooded over it for a moment with wicked intentness.

Then Blackie went back of the barn where the junk heap had accumulated for many years. Tin cans, broken wheels, worn-out plows, rotten harrow frames, shattered handles for pitchforks and shovels, and twisted refuse of a hundred kinds, lay here indiscriminately blended and melting together into an indistinguishable mass of ruin under the acid of time and weather.

It was a favorite place with Blackie. So ugly was this spot, so melancholy was its surroundings, so easy was it to think of failure, that no one else could be enticed near it, and when he wished for real solitude he was sure to find it here. He sat in the iron seat of an old gang plow and dropped his chin upon one doubled fist.

He must have absolute quiet now. In that silence he must develop and perhaps bring into being a great and daring plan. So his eye scanned the sweep of the hill above him, and saw it not, and his ear heard the firing of the 'shots' in the mine behind the great rock ledge over him, and heard it not. His mind was turned completely in upon itself.

In the first place, he knew that Connell hated him.

To be sure, when Connell died, as Mrs Connell had pointed out, he would be compelled by the law to leave part of his estate to his adopted son. But in the meantime, there were perhaps long years ahead during which Blackie would be at the mercy of his foster father. And during those years, how many acts of injustice and of cruelty would mar the life of Blackie?

He pondered darkly upon this unhappy thought. There were two great examples before him. The one was the way in which Connell had interfered to save Red when Blackie came home from school with his newly acquired knowledge of boxing. The other was the bitterly unjust fashion in which he had barred Blackie from enjoying the magnificent invitation of Greenough.

The second act was the decisive one. There might be some imaginable justice in the first act of the prospector; but to nothing but the darkest malice could Blackie ascribe the second. He had resolved upon vengeance at the time. He was more fixed in his resolve now.

And so the great thought grew.

While Connell lived he, Blackie, could be sure of a wretched life in which a thousand persecutions would be devised to make Blackie rue the day he was born.

What he most desired in this world was his own advancement. What he wished with only second intensity was the complete destruction of Red. And if that destruction could not be compassed, at least his impoverishment, his humiliation.

Suppose, then, that Connell were to die—were to be snatched from the world? Red would be left without a protector. More than this, Red would not be able to claim any part of the estate of Connell, for he had no legal claim upon the man—he had actually refused to establish such a claim. This thought continually staggered Blackie; he could not understand it. It was Greek to him of the obscurest nature.

But Blackie would be free to seek the Greenoughs. No doubt Mr Greenough would show a paternal interest in the orphan. A fine social life among ladies and gentlemen would spread before Blackie.

All of this was offered temptingly in the death of Connell. And suddenly the great thought struck home in the heart of Blackie. Connell must die.

CHAPTER TWENTY

PLANS ARE LAID

It turned him cold when it first was born in his mind. It brought him out of his seat with clenched hands and staring eyes. Connell must die.

Blackie moistened his lips. There was danger, great danger. If he were caught, what would happen? Not death, surely. For a boy of his age they would surely give a sentence of not more than a few years in some reform school. He drew a great breath and felt the warmth of his blood return to his heart.

His decision was fully fixed, now. Connell must die. But in what manner?

There was poison. There was that secret and terrible power which could be introduced in food and which could snuff out the life of the miner in a few moments.

No, poison would not do. There would be an autopsy and poison would be detected. He must have something equally sure, but which left a smaller trail behind it. Some common thing, perhaps. And why not a gun?

Men were less shocked when they heard of a killing by means of bullets. At least, they were less shocked in the West. A bullet wound through the head might mean, simply, that

164

some old enemy had come down upon Connell and had it out with him. And who that had hunted and mined through the West during many long and turbulent years, did not have enemies who wished his death?

The idea grew and took a firmer root in the mind of Blackie. A revolver would do the trick. And there were plenty of guns in the Connell house. And his own hand was trained and firm upon a gun butt.

He left the junk pile without a smile—cool, grave, determined. In his thought, Connell was already a dead man and he himself was already free.

The rest of that day he prepared the way. He made it his peculiar duty to be particularly friendly with Andy Connell. First he sought him out and told him that he agreed with Andy's conclusion about the Greenough invitation.

'After all,' said Blackie, 'I guess it's better. They're not my kind of folks!'

Andy was delighted. 'Blackie,' he said, 'the great thing about you is that you got hoss sense!'

Then Connell tapped the ashes and the cinder from his pipe and rose to go to the barns. It was an old habit of his, for every night before he went to bed, he made the round of the place and saw that the horses were safe, the barn door padlocked, and all living things under cover. He himself no doubt could not

165

have told what it was that forced him to make this round. Or he might have said: 'Injun days and Injun habits!'

In those old times, in fact, he had formed the foundation of this elaborate caution.

He had hardly left the house when Blackie rose and yawned, stretching himself with care.

'I'm sort of fagged,' said he.

'Bein' disappointed is pretty tiresome,' suggested Red with a malicious grin, and Blackie favored him with a single glance, wicked and secret as the glance of a snake's eyes. Then he went up the stairs to his attic room.

He had put the gun under his pillow early in the evening. Now he scooped it out, and the moment he felt the roughened butt against his palm, the consciousness came to him that he could do the deed and do it with ease. He looked down to the glimmering weight of the gun in his hand. And he knew that the last day of Connell's life on earth had come.

Then he went to the window. He had estimated the thing before. Just beneath the window the roof of the kitchen started and sloped far down toward the ground. He removed his shoes and slipped through. He kept close to the main wall of the house, and then worked his way down the outer edge of the roof. There the uprights gave the roofing a rigid support, but in the center of the roof there would be a greater chance for him to make a

166

creaking noise.

He gained the lower edge of the roof. He looked back and saw the back of the little window gaping behind him. He should have closed that window before he started, perhaps. However, it was not worth going back for now.

He dropped to the ground and started toward the barn. He had plenty of time, for the rounds which Connell made in these days were extraordinarily long, since he would not be contented until he had climbed up to the mine and searched around the shacks which stood near the mouth of it. On his way back, Blackie would encounter him.

It was ideal for his needs, the place which he found at last. Two boulders lay beside the path which had been worn dimly over the ground by these nightly trips of Connell up to the mine and back and by the many journeyings there and back during the day. Down that same path he was certain to come on this night again, for he was a man of the most methodical habits.

Blackie rested the barrel of the long Colt on the edge of the rock and sighted it. There could be no doubt that he would succeed in shooting straight when the time came. For when, in the starlight, he summoned up the imaginary figure of Connell striding through the night, he felt his heart grow stern and his forefingers instinctively crooked around the trigger of the gun.

Then something stirred behind him, a sound

167

like a breath of wind through a tree, but there was no tree near by. He whirled. And rising to his knees, the gun in his hand, his jaw set hard, he waited.

Nothing stirred. The rocks were surely not large enough to shelter any living thing of any size from his sight. And he decided that it must have been some small creature passing or, perhaps, unpleasant thought, a snake coiling its greasy length along!

He turned back, as steady as ever, and resumed his vigil. It was not long. For, presently, on the edge of the rock ledge he saw the bulky form of Connell against the farther stars. Down came the miner. He was singing quietly to himself, and his voice, even from a distance came with amazing clearness to the ears of Blackie:

> 'I was sick of bad fortune,
> I took to the road;
> My friends were unfaithful,
> I took to the road.
> To plunder the wealthy
> And relieve my distress—
> I bought you to aid me,
> My Bonnie Black Bess!'

Now he was close and closer. He towered a wonderful great height into the sky, so it seemed to the boy who was crouched against the ground. He drew his bead as he lay there; he drew it carefully, and his mark was the head of his victim. Just between the eyes he leveled the gun, his finger crooked firmly about the trigger, and then—upon his back dropped the weight of a falling body. The gun, thrown off its mark, exploded, and the familiar voice of Red sounded in his ear: 'You skunk! *You murderer!*'

That word turned him numb. He could not resist. He could not even rise to flee. Then the great hand of Connell found him and drew him to his feet, and there hung the gun in his hand. He could not even plead. The evidence, it seemed, was too utterly damning.

'Blackie and Red,' exclaimed the miner angrily. 'And you got one of my guns along with you?'

He snatched the weapon.

'By the heavens, it's one of my new ones. Who took that Colt? Blackie, I'm gunna skin you alive for this here. And I heard that slug whistle so dog-gone close that I figgered I was a goner for a minute! What in the devil does it all mean?'

The tongue of Blackie was paralyzed. He could not speak, not had his life depended upon a single syllable's utterance.

'Look here,' shouted Connell. 'I want to hear some talk. Darned if it don't begin to look to me as if—'

Then the voice of Red sounded. 'I can tell you, Mr Connell!'

Blackie turned sick.

'We come out here,' said Red, 'sort of to play Indian, d'you see?'

'Sort of to play the devil!' shouted Connell. 'But dog-gone me if I ain't too tired to give you a dressin' down to-night, Blackie. I'll serve you up good and brown to-morrow, though. Now the pair of you get back into the house and get into them beds as fast as you can!'

They fled together. They whisked into the house. And inside the door they paused and stared at one another, and there was astonishment in the eyes of both.

But in the surprise of Red was horror, and in that of Blackie was mere bewilderment.

CHAPTER TWENTY-ONE

UP AGAINST IT

He looked like a rat, and he was a rat. He had a yellow skin and a smoky black eye with yellowish pupils. His clothes were 'snappy,' with a Broadway cut, and the material was cheap enough to make a tailor see a profit. He wore dirty gray spats over shoes of scratched calf. He carried a stick and wore his hat rather far back on his head and pushed rakishly to the side. Perpetually he was fumbling for a cigarette and finding it, and holding the match

170

which he lighted until the flame seemed about to sear his fingers. Then he ignited the tobacco and snapped the match contemptuously away.

Such was Lew Bender as he arrived in Jackson Corners, and every man and every child in Jackson Corners knew at a glance that this fellow was 'bad medicine' with a vengeance. He looked, as Si Jenkins said afterward, like equal parts of rat and snake, and Si was right.

This was the man who asked where he could find Lewis Jason Connell. He asked it of Dan Harper, of the Circle Y Bar. And Dan spat in the dust before he answered.

'I dunno that I ever heard of a bird by that name. Say it over again, will you?'

'Lewis Jason Connell—'

'Connell? Andy Connell lives out on the road, but Lewis Jason? Why the devil, man, I have it now. You mean "Blackie!"'

'I've never heard him called that,' said Lew Bender. 'Maybe he packs that moniker in these parts.'

'Sure,' said Dan Harper. 'He don't pack no other. Might you be a friend of his—from back East?'

'Maybe I am,' said Lew.

'I seen Blackie around the corner; I guess that you'll find him there now.'

Lew Bender was glad to pass from under the searching, disagreeable eye of the stranger; he turned the corner and there his eye fell at once

171

upon none other than Blackie himself, reining a spirited horse and holding another horse by the bridle until presently a girl ran out from the post office and sprang into the saddle on the led horse.

He made a dashing figure on horseback, and when he presently dismounted, he was yet more notable on foot; for then one could see the careful workmanship which had been lavished upon the making of this youth. He stood, to a fraction of an inch, at exactly that romantic height which, it has been agreed, is neither too tall nor too short for a man. He was six feet tall in his stockinged feet. His face was such as one might expect to find, here and there, among the people of south Italy, dark, olive-skinned, and almost too handsome and smoothly perfect for the face of a man.

He was twenty-one years old. There was more fire in his eye than in the eye of the young stallion beside him. No girl in the world could have looked into his face and felt his eye upon her without a leap of the heart.

This girl was evidently no exception to the rule and smiled sweetly upon him as she turned to him. 'Are you sure that you can't come, Lewis?'

'I'm sorry that I can't.'

'You'll come over soon, though?'

'Of course, if I may.'

'Good-by, Lewis.'

'Good-by, Beatrice. Remember me to Mr

Greenough.'

She whirled away down the street on her horse; and Lewis Jason Connell, turning in the opposite direction, found himself almost on top of Mr Bender.

The latter leaned against a hitching rack, his feet crossed, one jaunty hand resting on his hip, and his broad, disagreeable smile was turned up toward the young man.

Blackie started violently: 'What brought *you* here?' he gasped out at the other. He added, without waiting for an answer: 'Didn't you get my last letter?'

'Was there a check in that letter?' snapped out Lew Bender.

'I explained in the letter,' began Blackie heavily, growing paler every moment.

'Was there a check in that letter?'

'No, but—'

'Then the letter wasn't worth waiting for. And I came back here to get some action out of you, young feller.'

Two or three people, in passing, eyed the stranger curiously.

'Let's get out of this,' suggested Blackie. 'I'll meet you at the end of this lane—'

He twitched his horse around, mounted, and galloped to the end of the cross lane. There was only one main street in Jackson Corners, and the town was so narrow and long, that a hundred yards from the pavement of the main street one could be out in the open again.

Under a broad old oak tree, Blackie got off his horse.

Mr Bender came toward this brilliant figure with a baleful expression and a sneering lip. He said, as he drew closer:

'Too good to be seen talkin' to me in the street, Connell?'

'Why should we stand out in the sun when there's shade here?' answered Blackie, but he flushed a little. 'Now tell me what's wrong. What brought you here, Bender?'

'Take it easy,' said Bender, and he sat down on a stump and removed his hat, so exposing a small head covered with hair which was well slicked and brilliant with vaseline. 'Who was the swell dame?'

'A friend of mine,' said Blackie vaguely. 'What I want to know—'

'I said,' remarked Bender, raising his voice harshly, 'who is the swell dame?'

Blackie bit his lip and flushed. 'She is Beatrice Greenough,' said he.

'The devil she is,' murmured Bender.

'Do you know her?' asked Blackie anxiously. 'Do you know who she is?'

'Sure I do. I've looked up the people around this burg. Her old man is the bird with all the spare millions. You ain't making a dead set at the Greenough dough, are you?'

'Certainly not,' said Blackie.

'Certainly not,' mimicked Bender. 'The devil, kid, lose it, will you? I know you, and I

174

know your kind. Cut out the bunk and talk straight to me, will you? It might do you some good!'

Blackie said not a word.

'Comin' back to the other thing,' said Bender, 'I want to know about the dough that you owe me.'

'I explained in my letter,' began Blackie nervously.

'Darn the letter. Lemme hear you speak your piece now.'

'Bender, I—I've struck rather on a rock—'

'You have, have you? A rock?' snarled out Bender.

'What I mean to say is—a temporary difficulty—'

'The devil, kid, talk out! You can't get the coin to pay me?'

'Bender, I'm frightfully sorry, but I can't. If you'll only give me time to turn around—'

'What's the matter with Connell himself? I've looked him up. He's got money to burn. What would two thousand be to him?'

'Two thousand!' exclaimed Blackie.

'Sure,' said Bender smoothly. 'It was fifteen hundred. When you wanted that money, I looked you up and made pretty sure that your old man had plenty of money to stand behind that. But I got to have the price of my ticket out and back and money for my time, too. That'll bring the fifteen hundred up to two thousand flat!'

'It's not fair!' groaned Blackie. 'Now that I'm down, you're taking advantage of me!'

'I say, why can't you get two thousand out of the old boy. Is he a tight-wad?'

'Bender, I'll tell you the truth: He gives me this allowance. He thinks that it's a big allowance. He looks back to the value that money had when he was my age. He doesn't see that times have changed. But if I asked him for more—'

'Well?'

'He's a Tartar! He'd laugh in my face! Besides, how could I explain why I need the money?'

'He's a Tartar, is he?' sneered Bender. 'Well, kid, I can be a Tartar, too; a darned red hot one, and if you can't explain how you come to owe me that money, I'll do the explaining myself. When he finds that you been playing the ponies—'

'Wait a moment,' broke in Blackie. 'Do you mean that you'd do that?'

'Don't I? I do!'

A yellow glint of danger came in the eyes of Blackie, and he looked so steadily upon the tout that the latter leaped suddenly to his feet and turned white.

'Look out, kid!' he gasped out. 'Don't do nothing foolish that you'll hang for.'

The hand of Blackie dropped away from his hip. 'I wish to Heaven that I'd never seen you,' he groaned.

'Well,' said Lew Bender, 'there's another way out. Suppose that you go to this friend of yours—this rich Greenough. Suppose that you go to him and tell him that you're in a hole. Wouldn't he kick through with the dough?'

'No, no!' shouted Blackie. 'Man, he detests gambling. I'd be ruined with him. It would be better to go to Connell.'

Lew Bender sat down on the stump again. 'That was what I wanted to get at,' grinned he. 'You and the girl are pretty thick, eh? Thick enough to get your hopes up?'

But Blackie merely bit his lip again.

'It has to be your old man, then? It's him that I have to talk to?'

'Listen to me,' said Blackie, in desperation. 'If you talk to Andy Connell, I'm done for. You understand that I'm only an adopted son?'

'Is that right?'

'It is. He'd pay the money, I suppose, but he'd put me down for a worthless dog. And he'd cut me off without a penny. That's his way!'

'A hard old bird, eh?'

'He's all of that.'

'Look here, Connell, I ain't such a bad guy. I've been in the hole myself, and I know what it's like. Well, kid, I'll give you a chance to turn around. I'll give you till to-morrow morning. But if I don't get the coin by that time, I go to Connell and spill the beans. Y'understand?'

177

CHAPTER TWENTY-TWO

THE WHITEST FELLOW

All the joy was gone from the heart of Blackie as he rode away from that oak tree and took the trail homeward. In a swirl before him he saw a thousand dark possibilities.

He would be unable to continue that courtship of Beatrice Greenough which, it seemed to him, opened golden possibilities for the future; possibilities far more golden than even the complete inheritance of the Connell fortune, even should that fortune turn out to be greater than Blackie suspected it might be.

His whole future, therefore, rested upon his ability to raise that sum of two thousand dollars—a paltry sum compared with his expectations, but to whom could he turn for it? Some money lender might give him that amount at a frightful rate of usury. But there were no money lenders near Jackson Corners—none of those gamblers in futurities, and he had only until to-morrow morning! Who else could he turn to?

He looked over the list of possible friends. But, indeed, what real friends had he? There were the Greenoughs, attached to him in the first place by a bit of sham in which he had taken certain credit which really belonged

178

entirely to 'Red'—there were the Greenoughs, but if he went to Chalmer Greenough with such a story as this, which he would be forced to tell, he well knew what the answer of the millionaire would be. Doubtless he would give the coin, but doubtless he would despise Blackie forever after. Even this, however, was better than to allow the tale to come to the ear of hard-headed, hard-hearted Andy Connell.

Many a year, now, the chiefest emotion in his life had been his hatred of Red. And yet, time and again, Red Hardwick, out of strange largeness of the heart which Blackie could not really comprehend, had come to his assistance. Still they remained what they had always been—rivals in everything.

It was in vain that Blackie had secured for himself the legal position of son to Andy Connell. The heart of the old miner, he well knew, was still as ever linked in affection to Red. And now, as a final touch, Red was beginning to show a great interest in Beatrice Greenough.

He had watched them at the last dance in the village; Red danced badly enough, and he talked little enough, but Blackie could see that he was happy with the girl, the girl happy with Red. Partly, no doubt, because of the stories of Red's football prowess in college. Though, for that matter, were there not far more brilliant stories to be told about Blackie, himself, on the gridiron? But, above all, she had been flattered

179

because Red, who never paid the slightest attention to any girl, had at last come to her feet among the rest of her admirers.

However, it was still possible that Red might do something for him. It was a weakness of Red's. He did not know how to say 'no,' and Blackie despised him for the very folly of the thing.

He found Red in the big new corral behind the Connell house taming a five-year-old mare which Joe Hooker had caught and given to him. She had run wild until this year and become as tough and as hardy as a mustang. Now she was a creature all fire and danger. Red had found an odd name for her, but it never seemed trite when one had the mare in sight, with her trembling, dilating nostrils, and her glittering eyes, and her wild beauty, and her ears twitching back and forth.

Spitfire they called her. Joe Hooker himself sat on the top bar of the fence and gave directions while Red worked. It seemed to Blackie a ridiculous and rather contemptible thing that an educated young fellow, such as Red, should submit himself to the direction of a rough cow-puncher like Joe Hooker. But there was Joe, using a specially caustic tongue on this day.

'Ease up the rope to her head— Is that easing up the rope? I didn't say yank her head off—I said ease up to her. Give her some slack, now, and start all over ag'in. You got a gentle hand like an Indian! Here you been working five days and making her worse every day. Steady, Red. Now go at her again. Not so fast; not so fast!

'The devil, kid; work like you had a thousand years to do it in; not five minutes. If you want to *break* her, go ahead with the rough stuff. But if you want to *tame* her, treat her like she was a lady, and a lady she'll be!'

Blackie could endure no more. He had an overwhelming desire to repay the puncher with some of the edge of his own tongue, but he restrained the impulse because he knew that it would anger Red more than it would the cow-puncher. Besides, if the latter were really irritated, he had a ready and a deadly gun.

So Blackie merely stepped into view around the corner of the barn and watched Red going inch by inch toward the head of the frightened, shaking mare.

'Red!' he called. 'I want to talk to you!'

'Can't you wait, Blackie?'

'It's important.'

'So is Spitfire.'

'I tell you, I mean it, Red.'

'All right, then. Say, Joe, will you try your hand with this fool mare while I talk to Blackie?'

'If you figger she's a fool,' said Joe Hooker coldly, 'I'll take her back and get you another hoss with more sense.'

'No, no, Joe. I wouldn't trade her for a
181

dozen of those whip-trained brutes.'

'Then do the training yourself. It ain't your hoss unless you've trained it yourself. Y'understand? It ain't your book unless you've wrote all the words in it.'

'All right,' sighed Red, submission itself. 'I'll come back and try you a little later, Spitfire.'

He came to Blackie, red-faced from his labors in the sun. The dust had mingled with the perspiration and streaked his face with mud.

With every year he had grown more and more unlike Blackie. Red was wider of shoulder, shorter, with long, dangling arms and the blunt jaw of the natural fighter. Now his blue eyes twinkled at Blackie.

'What's up, Blackie?'

'Red, I'm ruined.'

'The devil!'

'I'm flat, Red.'

He had made up his mind that no lie would serve his purpose as well as the truth.

'Flat? Is it really bad, Blackie?'

'Worse than you could imagine.'

'What can *I* do?' said Red, without too much friendliness in his tone.

'First give me your word that what I say to you stops with you.'

'Of course.'

'I'll take your hand on that, Red.'

'You're a suspicious devil!' said Red, and gave his hand carelessly enough.

Here Blackie breathed more freely, for he knew that the pledged word of Red was more binding than an oath sworn on the Bible by another man.

'Now let's have the story.'

'Red, last year in school I knew a chap from the South who used to make some money by playing the ponies—'

'I see. You tried the same thing and were trimmed. Is that it, old-timer?'

'Trimmed pretty deep.'

'Well, how much?'

'Two thousand bones!'

Here Red whistled by way of comment. 'That's the devil, Blackie.'

'And now the rat that got the money out of me in the first place has come on to Jackson Corners, and he swears that unless I get the money to him by tomorrow morning he'll blow the whole news to dad.'

'D'you mean it? It would finish you with him, all right. He'd cut you off like a mangy dog. How he hates gambling!'

'And you'd have the whole deal left to yourself, Red. It's hard to ask you to stand by me, when you stand to win everything and lose nothing—'

The thought made the face of Red flame. He dropped an impulsive hand upon the shoulder of Blackie.

'Darn it, Blackie, I'd never stand by and see you sink like that. But what can I do? Two thousand looks like a lot of money to me.'

'Haven't you saved anything? The old man is a lot more generous with you than he is with me.'

'I know that he is. Yes. I've got about seven hundred salted away. You can have that, of course. But that's only a starter.'

'And I can't finish the collection, Red. There isn't a friend I could borrow from except Greenough, and—'

'Oh, I understand. You couldn't do that—not if you were starving. Wait a minute, Blackie. I may have some friends who'll corral some coin for me. I could try them, anyway.'

'Heaven bless you, Red, if you could do that!'

'I'll do my best with them. But I don't know—I'll take a whirl at them as soon as I can get a saddle on a horse.'

'Red, you're the whitest fellow in the world!'

'Bunk!' grinned Red, touched by this praise, and whirled away to get a horse. Blackie sighed with vast relief, and then he smiled. After all, a fool like Red deserved to enjoy nothing but the fruits of folly and labor for others all the days of his life.

CHAPTER TWENTY-THREE

MONEY IS RAISED

When Blackie went back to the house, Red pondered the matter carefully. His problem was quite different from that of Blackie. For whereas Blackie had a thousand acquaintances and no real friends and no real enemies, Red had a thousand enemies and perhaps some score or two of friends who were bound to him, it might be said, with bonds stronger than steel.

Among those friends he could go as he would and ask what he chose to ask, but there was this great trouble. Most of them were poor men—as poor, say, as common cow-punchers and laborers are apt to be. For the best companions of Red Hardwick were not among the upper classes even of that rough community. The men he loved lived by their hands.

He went back slowly to Joe Hooker, who was still sitting on the fence, supporting his lean face between his hands and staring at Spitfire. She, rejoicing in the freedom from the hand and the rope of man, was gamboling like a mad thing through the little corral and raising a dense cloud of dust.

'Ain't it a shame?' remarked Joe Hooker.

'Ain't what a shame?' said Red, falling

sympathetically into the same vein of grammar.

'Look there at Spitfire. Don't she look like she was floating on a bubble of air? And here I've caught her and dragged her in where she's gunna be a slave instead of running free, out yonder. Ain't it a shame, Red?'

'I don't know that I've ever thought about it,' said Red.

At this, the cow-puncher turned his head and looked with a sort of sad reflectiveness upon his youthful friend.

'Look here, Red,' he said, 'with all the studyin' that you been doin' back East in that school, how much thinkin' *have* you done?'

At this Red, without a trace of pride or secretiveness, rubbed his chin and frowned as he summed up the total.

'Not a darn bit,' said Red. 'We get some books shoved at us, Joe. We grind through them. We memorize a bit. We get so we know what the professors want us to answer. They give us passing grades, and that's about all there is to it! The only thinking I've done in college, I guess, was out on the football field.'

'Why, Red, you might as well have been out here wrastlin' with steers and bulldoggin' the yearlin's.'

'I might as well,' admitted Red with perfect simplicity, so that Joe Hooker grinned broadly upon him.

'Darned if you ain't an honest man, Red,'

186

said Joe, 'and that's why some of us love you and some of us hate you. Well, kid, no matter what happens, you'll come out on top. Honesty wins.'

'Are you on top?' asked Red. 'And ain't you honest?'

At this, Joe Hooker scowled toward the distant horizon. 'Well,' said he, 'I guess that's thinkin' a jump ahead of me, at that. Besides, maybe I been honest, but I been mighty foolish, too. I've done my talkin' with bullets. And the last word that'll be said to me will be with bullets, too. Now what's ailin' you, Red?'

'I'm busted,' admitted Red. 'I'm flat, and I haven't the nerve to go to Andy Connell for any more dough.'

'Why not?'

'He's old-fashioned about money, you know. And what I need is too much. He'd figure out that I'd been throwing my life away. I need thirteen hundred dollars, Joe.'

'Is that askin' me for it?' said Joe.

'It is, old son.'

Joe Hooker grinned. 'You'd take me for an ornery maverick that didn't have a cent in the world, I guess?' suggested he. 'Well, kid, I can pony over eight hundred cold simoleons right pronto.'

'Good heavens, Joe. How've you managed to save eight hundred dollars?'

'Don't ask me no questions,' said Joe grimly. 'I got the money for you in my breeches pocket,

187

and here it is. You don't need to count it. Take my word that it's eight hundred dollars.'

He drew out a bill fold and handed it to Red. The latter had flushed a little.

'This is taking a pile from you, Joe.'

'Not half as much as I wish it was. Mind you, I ain't askin' how you come to run into that much debt—a kid your age—but I wouldn't mind knowing!'

'From being a fool,' said Red. 'I'll tell you the story some other day. Now I'm figuring who I can hit next.'

'Your next best friend,' said Joe.

Who was the next best friend of Red Hardwick, prospective heir to the largest part of the Connell millions? Red found him in Jackson Corners with the hind hoof of a work horse hooked up between his legs and resting upon his leather apron. The thick odor of burned hoof hung in the place, and little blue pools of smoke were gathered among the shadows of the upper corners; and broad streaks of sunlight broke through the generous cracks in the walls of the smithy, cleaving through the mist in the old shed.

'Hello!' said Red.

'Oh, darn your heart,' said the smith.

'How's things, Si?' asked Red.

'Now, blast you!' concluded the smith, and drove the last nail home, and rasped off the outside of the last hoof.

'I never seen such a way as the Cameron

boys keep their hosses,' said the smith by way of greeting. 'Darned if they don't come in here without a tatter of a shoe on any foot of their hosses. One hoss'll have his hoofs wore to the red. Another has 'em all growed out of shape, and I got to carve away like I was makin' a darn statue before I can find the foot to put the shoe on. Sit down, Red; and tell me what's what. Have you been boxing to-day?'

'No,' said Red.

'That's bad,' sighed Si Jenkins. 'When I was your age, I was working every day and working hard. It's *every* day's work that counts the most. And you need it—how you need it! That left of yours ain't no more straighter than the back of an old woman. You got a right cross like a greaser swatting flies. Oh, Red, you need a lot of training. When I was your age—why, you couldn't of put a glove on me. I would of stayed away out of the smash of that all-fire shift of yours—Lord knows where you found that punch, and I'd of pecked you to pieces with long-distance jabs.'

'Maybe you would,' said Red.

'Don't be so modest,' said Jenkins, 'when you know that I'm lying. What's the matter? Have you come to ask me for a favor that you act so dog-gone polite?'

'That's the long and short of it, Si.'

At this, the blacksmith sat up a little from the box of nails which he had chosen as a chair. He drew forth a handkerchief and with it

189

mopped away the soot from the fore part of his face.

'Well, well,' said he more gently, 'what could I be doing for you outside of teaching you how to hold up your mitts, kid? What could a sooty old fellow like me do for Connell's smart kid?'

And Red answered: 'You can do for me what Andy Connell would sweat a lot in doing. I need five hundred dollars. Joe Hooker handed me eight hundred a while ago. Can you hand me any part of the rest?'

'Five hundred simoleons,' said Si Jenkins. 'Ten thousand beers,' he translated. 'Well, kid, that's a lot of money for a gent like me to lay hands on. But I've laid away some coin. The old woman has it.'

'You can't ask it from her, Si. Not for me.'

'Can't I?' said Si calmly, the dangerous calm of one whom nothing can stop. 'Oh, but I can, though. You wait here!'

He rose and left the shop and when he was gone, Red made a wry face.

Presently Si Jenkins came back with a harried look which told how high the voices must have been raised in the house before he was able to extract the needed coin from his wife, but he counted into the hand of the youngster five hundred dollars in wrinkled bills.

'There you are, Red,' said he.

'You'll get interest for this,' said Red, greatly moved.

'I'll get the devil!' declared Si Jenkins with warmth. 'The interest I want is to see you practice with the gloves every day. Oh, Red,' he went on, stepping back again and eying the deep chest and the sinewy arms of the boy, 'when I think of what you might do in the ring if you was to give your mind to it, it makes me sad. Darned if it don't! But here you are with the makings of a middleweight champion in you, and here you are tied up to a bunch of money that old Connell is sure to give you. I say it's a sad thing, Red!'

'You never can tell,' murmured Red. 'I might come to it, Si. And if I do, you'll be my manager, eh?'

'Kid,' said the blacksmith solemnly, 'I'd make you champeen inside of a year. That's all. How's the footwork?'

'I'm jumping rope.'

'That's right. It'll keep you shifty and light on your toes.'

'So long, Si.'

'Does Joe Hooker know that Larry Rawson is in town?'

'The devil!'

'He is, though, and talking pretty black about Joe.'

'I'll tell him.'

'You better. Larry is a hard one. He says that Joe killed a cousin of his up in Montana last year.'

'Joe wasn't even in Montana last year.'

'You can't tell Larry that. So long.'

'So long. I'll pass the word along to Joe.'

He mounted his horse and cantered down the street, and Si Jenkins watched the dust trail hook out of sight around the next corner.

'What deviltry has he been up to now?' murmured Jenkins to himself.

* * *

It was hardly a scant five minutes after this that Mrs Tom Cuttle knocked at the back door of Mrs Sim Burton with a cup in her hand.

Mrs Burton presently opened the door.

'Have you half a cup of brown sugar, Mary?' said Mrs Cuttle.

'Sure I have. Come in and rest yourself while I get it.'

Mrs Cuttle sat on a stool by the stove, smiling politely, but her eye was filled with fire, and Mrs Burton saw it. She brimmed the cup with moist brown sugar and brought it back.

'You're makin' one of those wonderful coffee cakes that your Tom loves so,' suggested Mrs Burton.

'Humph,' said Mrs Cuttle. 'Yes, I am. If men take a liking to a thing, they never get tired of it.'

'Now, that's a true thing!'

'Dogs or whisky or both, when they take to 'em, they never leave 'em!'

'Dogs is a terrible nuisance,' was all Mrs

Burton could think of to help on the fray.

'Ain't they?' said Mrs Cuttle. 'That white devil that the Harkeys own, it took after my Tibby, a while ago.

'I went right out to get poor Tibby. The little thing was nearly frightened to death; and while I was trying to coax it down to me from the roof, it heard the voice of a man in Si's shop, and that voice frightened it back. I was sorry. Because while I was there trying to coax Tibby down, I couldn't help overhearing some of Si Jenkins' business, with young Oliver Hardwick!'

At last it was coming. Mrs Burton folded her arms and prepared to listen, but first she threw the door wide open, to show that all news was good news to her.

'I never thought much of Si Jenkins,' she declared, 'with his prize-fighting past! A very poor sort of a man to bring up children next door to. Speaking personal, I never go to see Mrs Jenkins more'n twice a month!'

'Nor me—not if I can help it. But that Hardwick—he'll come to no good end. He's a horrid fighting boy—a regular brute.'

'Well I guess that young Red Hardwick has enough trouble to last him for a time!'

'I hope not!' gasped out Mrs Burton.

'I kind of fear so!'

'Fighting will take young men into mighty bad trouble.'

'Fighting—and women!' breathed Mrs

Cuttle.

'Women!' gasped out Mrs Burton.

'What else could a young man want thousands of dollars for? I ask you.'

'That he couldn't ask from Andy Connell that's so rich and so foolish about that boy.'

'That's what I said to myself. What could it be that Red Hardwick was afraid to tell Andy Connell about, and Andy fonder of him than most men are of their sons! What could it be? Thousands of dollars, Mary!'

'Do you realize that we got a sort of a public duty to the women and the young girls of Jackson Corners, Miranda.'

'Mary, I suppose we have.'

'Ain't they got a right to be warned what sort of a snake this Red Hardwick is?'

'They *have* a right. There ain't a shadow of a doubt of that. Though what any girl could see in that ugly boy—'

'He's got the Connell fortune behind him. People say that Andy will be fool enough to leave most all of his millions to Red Hardwick.'

'I think we ought to call in Mrs Chandler. She's had more experience than we've had!'

'Call her in by all means! To think that your Tibby should have brought you to news like this!'

'I hope it will be the finish of that ruffian, Red Hardwick!'

And, by noon, a great heap of obloquy was raised towering above the head of poor Red

Hardwick, for it was now known and established by the busy brains of more than half the women of Jackson Corners, that he was a young reprobate who not only had been guilty with some innocent girl, but who also had run up great gambling debts.

CHAPTER TWENTY-FOUR

A GOOD SAMARITAN

It was the end of June, when the last of twilight and the first of dawn are only a stride apart, so that though the sky was already filled with the rose of the morning, no one was up when Lewis Jason Connell stepped out of the house of his adopted father.

Then he hurried on to the corral, caught a handsome brown gelding from the group of fine saddle horses which were kept there, and rode hastily toward Jackson Corners. By sunup, the way was half spent, and Blackie, singing as he whirled along at full speed, saw the blinding brightness of the sun strike on a wretched figure by the road.

It was a Mexican who had fallen far into bad fortune. He was young, indeed, but there was an old misery in his face—a sullen, lined, haggard face. One could see despair and sheer hunger in that face, and the eye which looked up to young Blackie Connell through a ragged black forelock was like the eye of a wild beast, filled with savage envy. He sat on a hump of earth by the road; there was not even a cigarette in his fingers.

Connell drew up in a cloud of dust. He was immensely gratified, for some reason, by the shocking face of poverty which he saw in this poor creature. If fortune had not come to his aid, he himself might have gone through his life as a pauper, and therefore becoming a drifter, a criminal unless luck befriended him. For he could look far enough and honestly enough into his own nature to see the weaknesses of it. The Mexican did not so much as glance up at him; not a word came from his lips in answer to the cheerful 'Good morning!' of Blackie.

'Here,' said Blackie. 'This will cheer you up!'

And like the king to the leper, he drew out no less than a twenty-dollar bill and tossed it fluttering toward the man. It fell unregarded in the dust before the feet of the man. No, not unregarded, for the man was turned to stone, and in his face there was an expression of utter astonishment almost as strong as terror itself.

Words would come in another moment. But Blackie did not even wait for the dirty hand of the poor fellow to snatch at the money, he loosed his rein and rode on again at a swift gallop. After all, he could well spare that twenty dollars when he had in his pockets two thousand dollars which had been given to him without security, merely for the asking. If Red ever strove to close in on him for the repayment of that money, he would find it a difficult collection.

So Blackie laughed to himself in the greatness of his spirits. He felt far less gratitude to Red than mere amusement over the folly of his foster brother. For who but the greatest fool in the world lends such a sum of money in cash without taking in turn for it a note of some sort? And now, such was his affluence, that he had been able to ride like a god into the life of another man, toss him with a careless gesture renewed hope in life, and then ride on once more without having felt the gift he had just made.

That was the real basis of his happy mood on this morning. Not the mere fact that he had in his pocket enough to pay the exactions of Lew Bender, but because he felt that these recent events went to prove, again, the invincibility of his cleverness. Only now and again, during his life, there swept over him a certain feeling of dread and a gloomy foreknowledge that fate would, eventually give to Red the great reward for his goodness and crush him, Blackie Connell, for the real evil in his nature. However, like many another sinner, Blackie allowed none of these thoughts to grow too great in his mind. And this morning, in particular, he felt that he sat on the topmost peak of the world.

When he reached Jackson Corners there was only a beginning of a stir of life, but the busy little village was almost silent. Only here and there smoke was rising from a chimney. It would still be an hour before the bulk of the housewives rose to their breakfast cookeries. And, in the meantime, the sun was already high and bright in the east.

At the hotel, he found the proprietor newly up, still unshaven, bleared of eye, and chewing with distasteful writhings of the mouth at a cigar butt of the evening before.

'Well?' he said to Blackie, speaking around the odorous butt.

'Show me the room of Mr Bender,' said Blackie.

The proprietor led him up the complaining stairway. 'You know this here Bender, I guess?' said he.

'Yes,' said Blackie, and he added defensively: 'Why not?'

'Why not?' said the proprietor, halting and squinting at his companion. 'Well, sir, everybody's business is his own business. I ain't askin' you for no free information, Connell. Only, I'd like to give *you* some.'

'Very well,' said Blackie coldly.

'You might step out and tell this here friend of yours—this here Bender, as you call him— you might tell him that we're mighty simple people in Jackson Corners, and there's a lot of things in life that we don't know nothin' about.

And particular you might say to him that there's a whole pile of things that we don't *want* to know about. Y'understand? And one of 'em is: How to talk to a pack of cards so's they answer back to your voice!'

He said this with a very significant sneer, and then guided his guest on down the hall to a door on which he knocked and then retreated. It was not until Connell had repeated that knock twice that he received a weak, groaning answer.

'Open the door,' said Blackie, trying the knob with a rude rattling. 'It's I.'

'Oh,' muttered the other, and presently the bed springs creaked, and then the floor quivered under his step. He opened the door with a jerk and waved Connell in.

'This is about the time that you start stirring around, I suppose? This is the average beginning of a day for you, Connell?'

'I've got the money,' said Blackie.

'What money?'

'I guess you've forgotten about it, eh?'

'Oh,' murmured the other, as the light poured in upon his brain at last. 'You got the stuff.'

He ran back to the bed and sat up against the pillows. Then, with nervous fingers, he reached for a cigarette, lighted it, and began to smoke with a jerky rapidity, blowing forth the clouds in strong puffs.

'All right, all right!' he snapped out. 'Lemme

199

have it, will you? Are you paying a visit, or money? But you're a good kid, Connell,' he went on more smoothly, changing his expression. 'You ran into a lot of bad luck. The ponies ran like a lot of fools when you started playing them. The next time, better luck. And believe me, kid, I can show you the way to the better luck.'

'I have the cash here,' said Blackie, too disgusted to prolong the conversation, and he handed from his wallet a great mass of compacted bills.

'All in chicken feed,' snarled out the tout. 'What in the devil's the idea? All chicken feed.'

He began to count the money with a lightning rapidity, simply letting the bills drift through his fingers, so it seemed. Presently he swept the crumpled heap together and glared at Blackie.

'Only seventeen hundred,' he snapped out.

'That's it,' nodded Blackie. 'I couldn't raise a penny more for you. That's your ticket out and your ticket back, and your fifteen hundred with a little left over.'

'What about my time?' snarled out the gambler. 'Ain't that anything? Am I a fifteen-a-week bum? Do I count for nothing? No, kid, I'm letting you off easy as it is. Go back and collect the other three hundred. You're an active boy, and you got a lot of hours before noon. I want that three hundred back here then!'

Blackie made a wry face and drew out his wallet with a sigh. 'All right,' said he. 'It's robbery, but you've had me under your thumb. Well, here's the other three hundred.'

The tout grinned broadly as he counted it. 'Trying to pull one on me?' he suggested. 'But I ain't a boob, kid. Not yet.'

'Another thing,' said Blackie dryly, 'and I'm giving this free. The boys are on to you already. You've been showing your hand too much, and if you want to keep good health, Bender, I advise you to drift along to new diggings.'

'Who filled you full of this line of chatter?' barked out the other, scowling.

'The proprietor. He's rather hard-boiled, Bender. And so are some of the others in the town. They don't like the way you make the cards talk.'

'A lot of tinhorn sports!' snarled out Bender. 'I didn't touch them for more than a hundred and fifty, last night!'

'No? That means a good deal in this part of the world. But it isn't what you do; it's the way you do it that counts out here. Take my advice and blow, Bender!'

The other shrugged the bedding higher around his narrow chest. 'I dunno,' said he. 'This ain't so bad. I figger this town is luck, for me. Here I am two thousand in, besides the chicken feed that I picked up from the boys last night. And maybe I'll be able to pick up some more stuff—here and there—here and there.'

201

He added: 'But if they try rough stuff, I'm the kid that eats it! I know their gun play. I ain't so slow with a gat myself. And where they keep bean shooters, I keep a hose.'

He pulled out a shining automatic. 'It sprays lead!' grinned Bender.

'I don't see what you gain by staying on here,' said Blackie with a sudden touch of anxiety.

'You don't?' chuckled Bender. 'When I find a goose that lays golden eggs, am I going to turn loose from it so quick you'd think that my hands were burned? Not me.'

A dull flush ran over the face of Blackie. 'You'll stay here to dig gold in me?' he asked.

'Don't be so rough, kid!'

'What have you over me?'

'Oh, I dunno. I might try talking to old man Connell, you know, and telling him a few yarns about what you do with your allowance. I'm not saying that I would, you know. But in a pinch, if I needed a hand-out and you were a little tight—I might try a line like that on Connell, kid. What would you say?'

CHAPTER TWENTY-FIVE

THE MEXICAN RENEGADE

There was, indeed, nothing for Blackie to say,

and he remained quiet, staring at Bender.

A shiver ran through the smaller man.

'Don't look at me that way, kid,' said the gambler. 'It gives me the willies. I ain't a snake. I'm just sensible. Put yourself in my place, and what would *you* do? I ain't gunna bleed you white; but only in case that I'm down and out, a man likes to know where he can put his hand on a—friend.' He brought out the last word with another grin.

'You mean blackmail as long as you can work it on me,' said Blackie. 'But, as a matter of fact, I think it's all a bluff. I think you wouldn't have the courage to face Andy Connell with your yarn.'

Bender shrugged his shoulders securely. 'Maybe you're right,' said he. 'But if you lay on that, you're betting long odds. Well, I ain't holding you up to-day, anyway. Run along and have a good time. Only, don't suggest that I leave Jackson Corners too quick. I like this place. Sleepy looking, but a lot stirring behind the face of things. Eh?'

Blackie went slowly from the room, and in the dining room of the hotel he ate his breakfast in dark and silent thoughtfulness. Now that he reviewed the whole matter he felt that he should have known in the first place what was coming. The ease with which the tout had bled his victim would keep The Rat on that trail.

Well, what would end it? After all, the story

203

Bender could tell was not such a damning enormity. But if it were told to Connell, with that man's strange semireligious obsessions and unreasonable prejudices against gambling, particularly gambling for young men, Blackie had few doubts of the result. It might be many years before Connell died, and during all of that time, The Rat would be a constant menace to the life, liberty, and happiness, so to speak, of Lewis Jason Connell.

Finally he got up and took his horse from the hitching rack in front of the hotel and passed on down the street, but all the joyous sense of superiority was gone from him. And he was still letting the horse blunder along, head down, on a loose rein, when a thrilling, cheerful voice hailed him suddenly.

He looked up and saw before him none other than the ragged Mexican to whom he had given alms. But how changed was the man! Indeed, his face was hardly recognizable. Half of the seams had disappeared. His head was carried high. The hungry look was gone, and the despair was gone, also.

His step was light, and the only sign that he was famished was the tightness of the belt that ate into his lean middle, drawn to the last hole. But the dust had been brushed from his clothes, his ragged forelock had been brushed back, and now, as he waved his hat and hailed his benefactor, he could have stood for a picture of a man crying: 'Gold!' or 'The

Promised Land!'

'Señor, señor!' cried he to young Lewis Connell. 'It is the blessing of God that I have been permitted to see your face again so that I may give you my thanks.'

'It isn't a matter for many thanks,' said Blackie mildly.

'To you, no,' said the Mexican. 'But to me, it is salvation. Consider, señor, that an hour ago the world for me was filled with cruel devils, not with men. That there was nothing left for me except to kill or to die like a starved dog. And now, señor, God had sent you to me to save me. He sent you to me like a part of the bright morning. God bless you forever.'

Blackie shook his head with a melancholy smile, and the expression of the Mexican changed to one of the most tender sympathy.

'Ah,' said he, 'your own happiness is gone. You have given it away to me with this money. Did you give me too much? Then take it back!'

He held out the bill, continuing: 'It is not the money which saves me, but the kind heart behind the money, my benefactor.'

'Keep it, keep it!' said Blackie hastily, ashamed of the impulse which had made him make a half gesture toward receiving back the alms. 'I am happy enough. Good morning, my friend.'

He would have ridden on, but the Mexican stood in the trail and barred the way with his arms eagerly stretched out to the side.

'I am your servant, señor. When my master is in trouble, what is my happiness except to serve him? And there is trouble in your face, señor.'

Blackie scowled gloomily down upon him. 'What is your name?' he asked.

'I am José Ridal.'

'José Ridal, have you had an enemy?'

'Ah,' said José. 'Do you see me now in rags, without even a horse to ride, with an empty pocket, with a starved belly? Yes, señor, I have had an enemy!'

The concentrated malice of a great hate darkened his eyes. 'I, too,' said Blackie, 'have an enemy!'

The Mexican's smile flashed eagerly.

'See, señor,' cried he, 'how God intended us for one another? You to save my life from despair and my own hands. I to find the enemy of my master and put my heel on the head of the snake! Is it not true?'

The malice in the heart of Blackie swelled in a hot wave into his very throat; and now he was looking greedily into the soul of the man before him. It was very true. The lean cut of that fighting jaw, the keen black eyes, the hawk nose, the light, athletic body, the long, nervous hands—all were the details which go to the making of a man of action. Here was one who would kill to-day and forget his killing on the morrow. Here was a man untroubled by a conscience. Suddenly, it seemed to Blackie that the overruling fates which controlled his life had indeed offered this man into his hand as a weapon to be used in this crisis, and why should not the thing be done? Was it not safe?

Certainly, if the thing were attempted and the Mexican were caught before or after the act, he would never open his lips to speak against his benefactor of that morning.

'If it is a man,' José Ridal was saying, 'only tell me his name. Do not tell me any more.'

As he spoke, he slipped his hand into his belt. There was a knife there; Blackie did not need to see the weapon with his eye; the suggestion was too strong.

'I shall tell you his name,' said he, 'but not because I want you to rid the world of the devil. He is Lew Bender, in Jackson Corners. If you find there a single human being who has a good word to speak for him—'

'He will be speaking about the dead before the night comes on this day,' declared the Mexican gravely. 'Señor Bendor is dead, and you, Señor—'

'I am Lewis Connell.'

'Señor Connell, think of this man no more. I have an assurance from heaven. It is not a sin to do this thing. It is intended; it is a necessary thing. And it is done. Adios, my master.'

'Adios, José.'

The Mexican whirled and passed him almost on the run, as he strode lightly off toward Jackson Corners, now lifting its roofs above

207

the depression in which it stood.

Who would ever have selected that gay figure as that of a murderer? But Blackie already could see the knife strike home. He shuddered a little; but then he shrugged back his shoulders. At the most, how could he be condemned for this thing? Even if the Mexican were caught and testified against him, what was the word of a Mexican renegade compared to that of the adopted son of rich Andy Connell?

But his spirits revived, now. As quickly as he had fallen into black depression, his heart now rose, and he let his horse break into a free canter, swinging him down the road toward the old Connell house.

From the distance he could see everything that was happening. Andy Connell was behind the house swinging the ax to cut up wood for the stove. It was a duty which he frequently had refused to turn over to either of the young men.

In the corral by the barn there was the inevitable Joe Hooker, who seemed to live and breathe only for the sake of being with Red Hardwick. Joe was now sitting on a fence and whittling wood while he watched Red work on Spitfire, and, certainly, Red had made great progress.

He was seated on the back of the mare—without bridle or saddle to help him—merely perched aloft on her bare back, securing her only with a twist of light rope around her neck and nose. He was soothing her with his hand and doubtless with his voice. So much Blackie could make out from the distance. Then, as he drew nearer, he saw the mare grow restless, saw her take a few dancing steps, then a flick into the air and Red rose in a high arch, tumbled head over heels in mid-air, and landed heavily on the corral, while Spitfire flaunted her heels high and fled to the far side of the corral.

'She's killed him,' muttered Blackie, half in horror and half hopefully.

But here Red arose and went staggering back toward the mare.

'He'll cut her to bits with the black snake, I suppose,' said Blackie.

But no, with extended hand Red went slowly toward the mare. Now he had cornered her again. Now he stood at her head soothing her. As if she had done a good act and needed a reward. Blackie shook his head.

He could not understand. No, he did not even want to try to understand such insane folly! So he pushed the gelding ahead. In the door of the shack stood Mrs Connell, the one congenial spirit that he found in his home, because they understood one another and need not play parts when they were alone together.

He came up to the house whistling, and Frederica Connell met him with a grin at the door. 'What deviltry have you been up to now?' she asked.

'Deviltry?' said Blackie, making his face

smoothly bland.

'Because,' said she, 'I've never known anything else to make you sing.'

CHAPTER TWENTY-SIX

SHERIFF GUERNSEY TALKS

The sun of that day gathered strength as it rose in the sky. Already by nine in the morning the temperature was eighty in the shade; it was eighty-five at ten, at eleven o'clock it was past ninety, and by half past eleven, it was verging toward a hundred. It was a dull, still day. Where the horse of Joe Hooker trotted down the street with sweat starting from every pore of its body, the dust rose from each step and hung in the air in separate little clouds, slowly dissolving; and when Joe stopped his horse in front of the hotel the dust cloud gathered thick around him and turned the hot, wet horse to a sudden gray.

First he gave the animal two mouthfuls of water and tethered it at the corner of the hitching rack, under the canopy of the shed which gave shelter from rain in winter and sun in summer. At this angle, whatever breeze arose would blow upon his mount. Then he climbed the steps of the veranda and picked out a chair in the line of idlers. He loosed the bandanna around his neck. He blew his own breath inside the enormous neckband of his shirt to cool his baked body, before he had recourse to the usual cigarette.

'Where you been, Joe?' asked a neighbor.

'Out to the Connell place.'

'What they doing?'

'In the mine?'

'Sure.'

'I dunno. I was with Red. The mine don't bother him none. He's riding a new hoss.'

'Is he good in the saddle?'

'He ain't bad. He can learn.'

'They say that he works out with you, using a Colt, every day. Going to make a fighter out of him?'

'Them that know *how* to handle a gun,' said Joc Hooker, 'is the ones that don't have no fights. Because they know that a gun pulling means a killing.'

A murmur greeted this announcement, and there was a sigh of answer from Joe, as though he realized that it would be impossible to convince these people, and therefore gave up the argument on the spot.

Here, however, a dust cloud appeared down the street and swept rapidly toward them.

'Who's fool enough,' said one, 'to ride a hoss like that in this sort of weather? Some fool kid, I guess.'

'Or, Sid Guernsey,' suggested Hooker. 'He's always in a hurry, dog-gone me if he ain't!'

211

The dust cloud dissolved as the stranger drew nearer. Then it was seen that it was indeed the sheriff, and many heads nodded and many eyes turned toward Joe in approbation of his insight.

The sheriff jumped off his horse and threw the reins. The poor creature was black with running sweat which washed away the dust as fast as it settled; it was trembling with excitement and weariness, and its flanks were stippled with red where the spurs of the sheriff had urged it along.

He was a little man, was Sheriff Sid Guernsey. He was about thirty, but a hard, active life full of burdens made him seem at least ten years older.

'Make Sid sheriff,' had been the cry two years before. 'He'll act like the county was a bank and he was the president of it.'

So they had made him sheriff, and he had lived up to every prediction. Nothing was too small for the attention of the sheriff. He not only apprehended criminals after their crimes, but he exerted himself chiefly toward preventing the crimes themselves. He was like the father of a family, and went around lecturing those who were in the process of becoming dangers to society. He became a sort of paternal tyrant, and the things he did could never have been upheld in a court of law. Now he ran up the steps of the veranda and stood there for a moment, turning his head with

212

quick little birdlike motions as he scanned face after face, nodding his silent answers to their greetings.

'You,' said he, suddenly cocking and leveling a forefinger like a revolver at the sleek, sporty form of Lew Bender, 'you, stranger, wear the name of Lew Bender, I hear?'

'I ain't had the pleasure of meeting you,' declared Lew Bender.

'You're lucky,' said the sheriff in his dry, snapping voice. 'I'm the sort that gents hate to meet, and I hate to meet gents. And I hope that I don't have to meet you, Bender. I'm Sheriff Sid Guernsey, if you're curious.'

'Hello, sheriff,' said Bender, changing color a little, but then, shrugging his shoulders, he added: 'You got nothing on me, old-timer.'

'I got nothing on you,' declared the sheriff, 'and I don't hope to have nothing on you. I hate trouble! Only, I been hearing that you get pretty friendly with the cards. Y'understand me? They say that you got a sort of an instinct for the cards. They talk to you—and you talk to them! Well, son, we hate that kind of language worse'n cussing in these parts. We like just one kind of talk. You remember that, and don't start forgetting it. That's all!'

He turned his back on Bender and walked with his quick, jerky step to tall Joe Hooker and stood right over him, with forefinger cocked and pointed again, like a gun.

'Joe, I hear that Larry Rawson is in town!'

213

'Maybe you do, and maybe he is,' said Joe Hooker, yawning. 'But I ain't seen him.'

'You don't have to tell me that,' said the sheriff. 'If you met up with him, I'd of heard the guns talking about it. Now, look here, Joe, I've got this to say: If you meet up with Larry and there's a fight, I ain't gunna listen to no talk about self-defense. I'm gunna take you to the lockup and put you in. And I'm gunna see that you get a trial before twelve gents that ain't your friends. I'm gunna see that you're tried for *murder*, Joe.'

'You talk,' said Joe, 'as though I was sure to fight with this fellow and as if I was sure to kill him if we *did* fight.'

'That's what'll happen. Rawson is here after you, and you know it.'

'If Rawson's in danger, then go tell him. *I* ain't hunting for him.'

'I've told him. But Rawson's a hard-headed fool. He's too young to know any better, and you ain't. Joe, I want you to up and leave Jackson Corners for a few days.'

Joe Hooker growled deep in his throat. 'I'm to side-step this here Rawson, am I?' said he. 'Sheriff, you're all right, and I'm for you. But you can't go too far with me!'

'All right,' said he. 'You got the right to stay here in town. But if you meet up with Rawson—'

'Ain't he a growed-up man? Ain't he got sense? Can't he handle a gun as good as the

214

next man?'

'He's all those things, but he ain't sure death and poison with a gun the way you are, Joe, and you know it. And if you kill Rawson, I'll make Jackson Corners the hottest place for you that you'll ever meet up with till you go to the devil. Y'understand me?'

But Joe Hooker's temper had been growing every moment, and now his face was livid; yet the voice with which he answered had grown very soft.

'You've said your little piece,' he declared. 'Now just step out and set down and rest yourself. I'm tired of listening to foolishness. I don't need no lessons in manners.'

For a moment the sheriff still stood over him, his face working, but then he decided that words would, indeed, be wasted in this place. He turned upon his heel and walked straight into the hotel, leaving a thick blanket of silence behind him. Even the wiping of perspiration from dripping faces was done with furtive movements, and the men looked at one another askance, like pupils in a schoolroom after the teacher has spoken words of stern reproof.

The first to stir was Lew Bender, who rose from his chair muttering: 'Aw, the devil—what a guy!'

He received no response, however, and so he strolled off the veranda and into the scattering shade of the pine trees near by; and almost at

215

once, the young Mexican rose also, snapped his cigarette out into the dust of the street, and went leisurely in the same direction that Bender had taken among the trees.

When he was well out of sight of the hotel, however, and deep among the trees, José Ridal stepped behind a sapling and snatched out a revolver. He looked to it carefully, swiftly, seemed to make sure that all was well with its working parts, and then put it away in his clothes again.

Presently he started on, and after a moment he came in sight of Lew Bender, who was walking slowly among the trees, pausing now and again to kick a pebble out of his path. Evidently all was not well with Lew Bender, and he needed something on which he could vent his emotion.

At that thought, the Mexican smiled with a mirthless enjoyment of the thing before him. Here he saw the gambler lean over and pick something from the ground, and as he did so, his clothes being drawn taut, José Ridal saw the outline of a gun stamped clearly in the back trouser pocket of Bender.

At this, he smiled and nodded again, and then hurried after the other until Bender turned at the sound of the approaching footfalls.

'Well?' said Bender.

'I have a message for you, *amigo mio*,' said José Ridal, 'and here I have found you alone
216

which is the best place for you to learn what I have to say.'

CHAPTER TWENTY-SEVEN

THE GUN FIGHTS

In the meantime, on the veranda of the hotel, the silence which the sheriff left behind him continued for a time uninterrupted, flowing like a dismal river through the minds of the men. They glanced at one another and they turned their eyes at last to Joe Hooker. At length it was decided by one of the older men that the talk should be turned on something else.

He got up and took a chair nearer to Joe.

'The sheriff is going too darn far,' broke out Joe hotly, mistaking the meaning of this approach.

At this, his companion nodded without enthusiasm and let his eyes follow a spinning whirlpool of dust which was walking down the street, though no breath of wind was felt along the hot veranda.

'The darn flies!' groaned Joe's recent companion, slapping at his ankles. 'They get teeth like bulldogs in days like this. Darned if they ain't a hungry lot and a brave lot! What's this news that I hear about your friend, Red

217

Hardwick?'

'Bad news, is it?' asked Joe gloomily. 'Nobody ever asks to hear any news about the good things that happen to you or to your friends. Well, what's up?'

The other lowered his voice. 'It's the yarn that they're passing around town.'

'What yarn?'

'About the trouble that he got into.'

'I don't know about no trouble.'

The other smiled wisely. 'Sure, you'd keep mum. But it's too bad, ain't it?'

'What's too bad? Don't talk so mysterious.'

'Why, about the girl that—'

'Red and a girl?'

'I dunno except what everybody says—and about how he went around borrowing money from everybody to get out of his scrape. He got to you for about a thousand, somebody was telling me, or was it two thousand, Joe?'

Joe Hooker snorted with rage.

'It was not,' said he. 'I never said that he borrowed a cent from me. The other yarn about him is a lie, too. I know Red, and I know what goes on inside of his head. He ain't that kind, and you can put up your money on it. And,' continued Joe with violence, 'some of these birds that are talking about him will run into a pack of trouble if Red comes to the lee side of what they're saying!'

The other grew blankly silent. 'I'm only telling you what I hear—' he began.

'Some folks,' said Joe bitterly, 'have got the sort of ears that pick up rotten bad news. They're like buzzards. They live on dead things, and they watch the dying things.'

A voice spoke up suddenly from the far end of the veranda—a voice half subdued but with a startled note in it that reached every ear:

'Rawson, by the heavens!'

And Larry Rawson himself came swinging slowly up the street, a tall, handsome young fellow, very brown of face, very cheerful of eye. He came straight toward the hotel, and at his coming, men suddenly began to rise from either side of Joe Hooker and move away.

Something was expected of Larry, and he saw instantly what he would have to do if he wished to call himself a man thereafter in the West. But, in that moment, he cursed the 'redeye' and the looseness of tongue which had made him repeat, with bitterness, certain dark things that had been rumored about the tall gun fighter in the last letters he had from his relations in Montana.

Yet, however much he might doubt the outcome of this engagement, he did not for an instant hesitate. His course was clear before him; he had a thing to do, and he knew just what that thing must be. So he went straight to tall Joe Hooker and stood above him, with an unsmiling face.

'You're Hooker,' he said.

'I'm Joe Hooker,' admitted the cow-

219

puncher.

'D'you know me?'

'I guess I know you. You're Larry Rawson.'

And then Joe made the greatest step, perhaps, that he had ever made in his life toward solving a difficult situation without the use of violence.

He said: 'Sit down, Rawson, and tell me how things are with you. Set down and have a smoke.' And he held out the makings.

Now, for a vital instant, Larry Rawson hesitated. He wanted with all his heart to accept that smoke and sit down with Joe Hooker and tell him, frankly, all that he had heard, and let Hooker defend himself from the imputation if he could, but the battery of many eyes of strangers was upon him, and, no matter how he yearned to do as he was bidden, he forced himself to shake his head.

'I'd like to do it, Joe,' he admitted. 'But before I can do that, I got to have a little talk with you about some things that I've heard.'

Joe Hooker tucked the makings back into his vest pocket. 'All right,' said he. 'Lemme hear what you got to say, Rawson.'

'You was up in Montana last year?'

Joe Hooker pushed back his hat and scratched his head.

'I dunno that I was,' said he. 'Well, I was up through Idaho—no, I guess that I didn't get across the border into Montana. Why?'

Rawson had turned a dark red.

220

'You never seen the town of Somerset in Montana?' he asked sharply.

'No,' drawled out Joe Hooker, still in thought. 'I never seen the town of Somerset.'

Rawson laughed harshly. 'And you was never seen there by any of the boys, I guess?' he added.

Hooker shrugged his shoulders. 'I dunno what anybody seen—or thought that they seen.'

'Maybe it was your ghost,' suggested Rawson with an increasing bitterness.

Hooker said not a word.

'Because,' said Rawson, 'it's sort of queer. I'll tell you what happened. My cousin, Dan Rawson, the finest kid and the squarest shooter that ever throwed a leg over the back of a hoss—he was in his shack in Somerset cookin' his supper. The neighbors seen him through the window, walkin' back and forth. And then they seen somebody go up to the front door and walk into the cabin. And after a minute, they heard a gun go off—not two guns, but just one gun!'

'Ah?' murmured Hooker.

'You don't remember nothing?'

'I'm hearing you talk, Rawson, I'm not remembering nothing, or I'd do some talking myself.' This with some asperity.

Larry Rawson moistened his dry, trembling lips and went on: 'Then a gent was seen running out of the house and down the street—

221

and some of the boys that seen him run, they said that he had the look of you, Joe Hooker!'

The tremor of his lips had become a tremor of his entire body. Then he added with a strained, deep voice of pain: 'When they come into the house, and when they looked for poor Dan, where did they see him? Over by the sink, on his face, with a bullet through his back—he'd been shot in the back!'

'Wait a minute,' said Joe Hooker. 'What time of day was it?'

'It was the evening; Dan was cooking his supper, just the way that I been telling you.'

'It was sort of dark, was it?'

'I dunno.'

'Was the lamps lighted?'

'Yes, they was. It was by the lamplight that they seen Dan walking around in his kitchen.'

'Look here, old son, if it was near dark, how'd it happen that the boys was able to recognize me as I was running down the street?'

It was a puzzler for Larry Rawson. And, though his mind had been more than half made up during the recital of the tragedy, he found himself fumbling, now, and unable to make any answer.

'Only,' he said, 'you ain't a man that looks like other men, Hooker. You ain't the same kind. It ain't likely that folks would mistake you for another. Sam Hewitt, he passed right by on the street, and he said—'

And, at this instant, at the very moment

when an amicable agreement seemed about to take place, fate intervened cruelly. From the grove of pine trees which circled the Jackson Corners hotel on the one side, two revolver shots barked across the heavy air of the midday, two shots chiming almost as one. Then on the heels of that noise came a scream of agony, of fear, that was cut away and died suddenly in the midst of the cry, as though a hand had been clapped across the lips of the tortured man. And no one who heard it needed to be told that the hand was the hand of death.

And the shots and the cry made Joe Hooker bound to his feet—made Larry Rawson start back with a cry: 'Hooker, you're a murderer!'

'You lie!'

'And here's paying you back in full.'

Larry Rawson was no novice. His gun came into his hand as a lightning flash comes into a storm-darkened sky; and yet, before he could press the trigger, the gun of tall Joe Hooker had spoken.

Rawson, shot through the body, slumped heavily upon his side to the floor of the veranda. He raised the gun for a final effort, but Joe Hooker kicked it from the half-numbed fingers. Then he leaped for the street and his horse at the same instant that the shrill, sharp voice of the sheriff within the hotel began to scream: 'Stand back—let me out—there's some devil's work going on!'

Joe Hooker was in his saddle by that time

and flying down the street as the sheriff burst through the tangled crowd in the doorway of the hotel. He saw the fugitive disappearing in a mist of dust down the white street; he saw the wounded man and leaped to him.

'How are you, Rawson?' he snarled.

'It was a fair fight,' gasped out Rawson. 'He beat me fair. I made—the first move—Lord!'

His eyes closed, and then he lay still.

The sheriff did not wait to make sure that his man was dead. He turned with a scream of rage and grief on the others.

'You murderin' cowards!' he shouted at them. 'I'll have Joe Hooker for this. You hear me swear it—and I never leave his trail until I've got him. Never!'

CHAPTER TWENTY-EIGHT

RAWSON HAS HIS WAY

No one could be blamed, at such a moment, with such a gun fight under their eyes, for failing to give heed to another tragedy not a hundred yards away where, among the little second-growth pines which the hotel owner hoped, on a day, would supply him with firewood, lay Lew Bender on his face with his arms cast out before him, each hand loosely filled with pine needles as he had gripped at the earth in his brief death agony. No one thought of Lew Bender then; and it was only afterward that Mrs Tom Cuttle could remember how she had seen the form of the Mexican as he skulked out of the wood at the rear of the hotel.

He went quickly toward the corrals behind the building, and, while half a dozen other men worked there, saddling their horses and then rushing away to follow the sheriff in his pursuit of the first criminal, José Ridal found an old tattered saddle in a shed, and a little, ugly, roach-backed, lump-headed mustang. He saddled that horse, for he saw in it certain qualities of toughness which, as he guessed, might stand him in very good stead in the days which were to come. Thus equipped, he patched up a broken bridle, and well after the main hue and cry had poured out of Jackson Corners on the trail of the luckless Joe Hooker, Ridal left the town in a different direction and headed straight for the northern hills.

Southward lay his own land and his own people, but to return to them, for certain very strong reasons, would be putting a noose around his neck—or, more likely, sliding a knife between his ribs. So he rode north, wondering in his heart of hearts at the strange Providence which had provided such a diversion and carried the wrath of the keepers of the law upon other heads at the very instant when he committed his crime. No one followed him. He presently had the trail to himself and let the mustang jog comfortably along it.

He seemed, indeed, to be jogging without danger out of the picture; but he himself knew that the danger was gathering more terribly than ever around him, no matter how far removed it might be. For, on that day, he had become not only a man slayer, but a horse thief also, and he knew that for either crime there was only one approved penalty among the rough men of the mountain desert.

But, while the Mexican journeyed north, secured for the moment from trouble, and deliciously conscious of sixteen dollars and plenty of tobacco in his pockets, new things were happening at Jackson Corners, and the chief of them concerned young Larry Rawson.

The doctor, when he first saw the wound and leaned over the youngster, simply said aloud: 'A goner! The boy is dying; he won't live five minutes. He ought to have been dead five minutes before this!'

That was the last important tidings of Rawson which the late riders from the town carried out to the sheriff where he was toiling on the trail of Joe Hooker. Rawson, they announced, was dead.

'Now,' said the sheriff to them, 'are you willing to shoot, and shoot to kill when you sight Joe Hooker?'

And they admitted that they were. It was not that the thing had not been a fair fight. Rawson, in a way, had forced the fight upon

Hooker; but Joe was too old a hand, and these gun-fighting stories had been told about him too often.

In the meantime, with the infinite strength of youth, Larry Rawson, back on the veranda of the hotel where he had first fallen and where his blood had first made the crimson smear on the porch, had sighed, groaned, and opened his eyes.

But they were dull eyes, and the lips which had framed the sigh hung limp and lifeless, agape.

'That's the death struggle of poor Rawson,' said the doctor.

'His eyes are open,' whispered an awed onlooker.

'Why, youngster, the eyes of a man always open when he dies.'

'You lose,' gasped out a choked and whispering voice from the floor of the veranda. 'I ain't dead.'

The doctor was properly taken aback. He looked, for an instant, as though he were hearing a voice from the grave. But he dropped on his knees beside the sufferer and took his pulse with skillful fingers.

'Rawson,' he said, 'I'm sorry to tell you that you are not long for this world. You are about to die, young man, and—'

'You lie!' gasped out the young cow-puncher. 'I got—fifty—years of livin' ahead of me! And—I'm gunna live—to clean up on that

227

Hooker.'

The doctor could not help grinning. 'All right,' said he cheerfully. 'If you say that you're going to live, Larry, you are. If that bullet twisted its way through you without tearing your vitals to bits, you *will* live. But if it *did* go through without killing you, it's a trained bullet and you ought to save it for a charm. Now, son, keep your mind fixed on that: If you say that you can live, you *can* live, and I'm going to help you out.'

So he had them lift young Larry Rawson and bear him into the hotel, very gently, very tenderly. Twice the youth fainted; twice he recovered his senses and groaned with agony before they put him on a bed on the first floor of the hotel.

'That young man will take a good deal of licking, and a good deal of killing,' said he. 'But—what the devil could that bullet have done to *avoid* killing him?'

Then he went to work to save this man who refused to die. There were more nurses volunteering than could be used, and every moment more were arriving. The doctor established two sensible women. One was to see that his orders concerning food were carried out to the letter. One was to see that the nursing instructions were carried out with a similar fidelity.

On the second day Doctor Chandler Marrow was forced to announce that he himself began to have some slight hopes. On the fourth day he declared that since the young devil had lived this long, he would be *surprised* if Larry Rawson died. And, on the fifth day, Larry Rawson opened his eyes and blinked at the ceiling with a perfectly clear mind working behind those eyes.

'Chief,' said he to the doctor, 'tell me in the first place what's become of Joe Hooker?'

The doctor shook his head. 'You think about yourself,' advised the doctor.

'What,' exclaimed the wounded man in a louder voice, 'has become of Joe Hooker?'

'Steady! Steady!' said Doctor Marrow. 'Keep still and I'll tell you everything I know which is, simply, that since the sheriff and about twenty of the boys dived into the hills five days ago, we don't know what happened.'

'The sheriff is after him, then?' asked Rawson.

'Of course. Like a bulldog.'

'It's too bad,' sighed the stricken man. 'Does old Guernsey know that I'm not killed?'

'How could we send him news when we don't know where in the mountains to find him?'

'He's got to be found,' said Rawson through his gritted teeth. 'Who has gone out to trail the sheriff?'

'Nobody that I know of.'

'Tell them to get some one. They'll find money in my clothes to pay his expenses.

Otherwise, the sheriff will catch up with Joe and Joe will never surrender till he's dead, and—'

'I see,' murmured the doctor. 'You want to save him for your own gun later on—you want to get laid on your back again? Well, son, the next time *would* be the end for you.'

'Oh,' muttered Rawson, 'I don't know about that. But I've lain here thinking, all the time, and every time I think about Joe Hooker I understand better that I was wrong. A man that would stand up to another man the way that he stood up to me, ain't the sort that would shoot a fellow through the back. Am I right, doctor?'

'You're right, and darned right,' admitted the doctor heartily.

'Then get somebody on the trail to carry the good news about me to the sheriff—and let 'em tell the sheriff what I think about Joe. That tall, skinny guy is straight!'

'We'll do it,' admitted the doctor. 'We should have done it before. Because now it'll be a hard job to catch up with the lot of them. They've gone a long way into the mountains; and Hooker and young Red Hardwick are not the kind who stand still in one spot, very long.'

'Hardwick? Good heavens, how does he come with Hooker?'

'Hush up. You've talked enough. I'll tell you the rest to-morrow.'

And the other, with a submissive groan,

closed his eyes.

CHAPTER TWENTY-NINE

TREACHERY AFOOT

Fate was still working into the hands of young Blackie Connell. In order to understand, we must go back to the day of the double shooting—the shooting which left Larry Rawson desperately wounded and much cared for, and Lew Bender dead and utterly unregarded.

But, in the meantime on that eventful day, Red Hardwick had continued to work over the gallant mare, Spitfire, until at last she allowed him to sit on her back and guide her gently and smoothly around the corral merely by the pressure of the rope against her neck. And he began to understand, now, that the reason she had fought against him was not really hatred, but simply a consuming fear of the damage that might come to her at the hands of this man if she submitted herself to him. The instant he came to understand that he was dealing with dread and not with malice, it seemed to the sweating, much-bruised Red, that he had opened a door to her inner nature with a key of magic. After that, he was able to do as he pleased. It needed only a great deal of

231

gentleness of hand and of voice, and she responded soon enough.

Yes, and when he had dismounted, and Blackie appeared around the corner of the barn, the mare, starting at the sudden appearance of the stranger, jumped close to Red as though for protection. Blackie swore with surprise.

'She's eating out of your hand at last,' said he. 'I never thought that you'd do it, Red!'

'Neither did I,' sighed Red, while he stroked her sleek neck. 'But she's worth the trouble, eh?'

'She's a beauty. Red, I came out to tell you something else.'

'Well, Blackie, what's the bad news now?'

'You've guessed right. It's bad news, and very bad news. That old fool, Mrs Munding—'

'I know her. She's the one who sent for the sheriff when we stole her watermelons—'

'That's the one. She showed up to-day—left about five minutes ago—with a long yarn about some stuff that she's heard in town— about you, Red, going around borrowing a lot of money because you—'

'Where the devil did she hear that?'

'I don't know. Would Hooker or Jenkins tell?'

'Never in a thousand years! It was some one else. Who could it have been?'

'I can't guess. You may have been overheard by some one talking to Joe or Si.'

'That must be it.'

'The worst of it is that they hitch another rotten thing up with the money. They say that you've gotten into trouble and that you had to get the money or go to jail.'

'The devil! How does the old man take it?'

'Connell is crazy. He's walking up and down the house swearing that it's a lie, but if it's true, he'll throw you out of the house and never look at you again.'

Red bit his lip and turned white.

Blackie hastened to add: 'Of course if it comes to a pinch, I'll step in and confess everything.'

'Only in the worst sort of a pinch,' said Red. 'I love the old man, Blackie. It would break my heart to fall out with him completely.'

'You love him, and I suppose you don't care a rap about his money?' suggested Blackie dryly. 'Well, come along with me. He sent me out here for you. He's pretty hot, Red. Think up something as you go along!'

'I've got to admit borrowing the money, I suppose,' said Red.

'I don't see why.'

'Because I could not lie well enough about that to get away with it. I'll tell him it was for a friend—I've got to tell him something like that.'

'Red, he'll corner you.'

'You trust me,' said Red. 'I'll hold out to the last ditch. I didn't go through all the trouble for

233

you yesterday, Blackie, for the sake of turning you down to-day.'

They went back to the house in a strained silence. And at the door they looked in on Mr and Mrs Andy Connell in the kitchen—she fussing vaguely at some dish of fruit which was stewing on the stove—Andy himself in his shirt sleeves seated behind the table with his elbows resting upon it, his thin, silver hair bristling up in every direction to tell of how his fingers had been thrust through that hair time and again in his excitement. His face, in which age appeared in the drooping eyelids, was brightly flushed, and he stretched out both his calloused hands to Red.

'Red,' said he, 'Blackie has told me the whole lying yarn. Now you tell me the truth!'

Red hesitated only an instant. 'I don't know how a lie like that could have started,' said he.

'It's all just malicious lyin', ain't it?' cried old Andy Connell eagerly.

'It's a lie and a big lie, all right,' said Red. 'I suppose somebody started it for a joke.'

'I knew it!' cried Andy Connell, sinking back in the chair. 'Oh, Red, if I'd a thought that you done a thing like that—the sort of a crime that they tell about—so's you didn't have the nerve to come to *me* and ask for help, but had to borrow from your friends, I'd of plumb died, Red, if anything like that had happened.'

Blackie flashed a glance of relief at Red, as much as to say: 'It's over, Red, and thank

Heaven for it!'

But here Mrs Connell, who did not appear so well pleased with the quiet termination of the affair, said gloomily: 'Seems to me, Andy, that it's mighty queer that there should be such a lot of smoke where there ain't no fire at all.'

'You women,' said her husband sternly, 'hate Red so's you can't help but wish him harm. But I tell you that that sort of a thing ain't in him.'

Here she turned upon Red. 'Red Hardwick!' cried she. 'Can you say that you didn't borrow any money from Si Jenkins and Joe Hooker—to say nothing of any others?'

The denial came up in his throat and stuck there.

He had to admit: 'I got some money from them.'

Andy Connell was struck gray by the admission, and Blackie winced.

'You *did* get money!' cried Mrs Connell. 'I told you that there was fire behind all of that smoke!'

'Red, you got money for what?' asked Andy Connell in a shaken voice. 'How much money did you get?'

'I got—quite a bit!'

'You got quite a bit?' echoed the miner. 'How much!'

'Thirteen hundred dollars,' said Red, his head falling.

'Thirteen hundred dollars!' shouted

Connell. 'For what? For what could you want a—a fortune like that?'

'For a friend,' gasped out Red, turning whiter as he saw the ridiculous imputation.

'For a friend?' repeated Mrs Connell, and broke into shrill laughter. 'Red, don't talk like a fool. If you're gunna tell a lie, tell a good lie.'

Andy Connell had hurried around the table and now stood before the boy, his face working with a great emotion.

'Red,' he said, 'for Heaven's sake tell me the truth. You know what you mean to me, Red. You know that what I got I hold more for you than I do for myself. I ain't wanted you to get the habit of a spendthrift. That's the only reason I don't give you fifty thousand a year to spend. That's the only reason, Red. Will you believe me? And if you had a friend that was in a hole, why didn't you come to me and tell me who he was and what he wanted? Wouldn't I of give the money to you as quick as a wink? Red, come out and tell me the straight of everything.'

Red cast a desperate glance at Blackie, but the latter studiously avoided the appeal.

'Answer up,' begged Connell. 'A straight answer is the answer that comes the quickest.'

'There's nothing that I can say,' murmured Red. 'Except—if you had known for whom I wanted the money, it would have made you angrier than to have me ask it for myself.'

Mrs Connell laughed again. 'That's likely,'

said she, sneering broadly.

'Red,' said Connell, with a flash of open anger, 'who was the man? Could it have been Blackie, here?'

Red started to speak a denial, but he could not make the words come.

'Blackie!' shouted Connell. 'By the heavens, I might of knowed—'

But, as he himself faced the youngster, he found that his suspicions were brought to a sudden halt. For the face of Blackie was the face of a master actor. Only astonishment appeared there at the first, and then astonishment was supplanted by bewilderment, by anger, by injured virtue.

At last he said sadly: 'Red, why do you stick a knife in me, when I haven't harmed you?'

'Oh, the wicked young devil!' exclaimed Mrs Connell.

But in Red, rage and wonder took the very face of guilt. For he grew white, and his lips trembled, and his eyes started from his head.

'Guilty!' groaned Andy Connell. 'Oh, Red— Red, if you got anything to say—if you got any word to speak, speak it now.'

'Blackie!' cried Red in his agony.

'I'll do what I can,' said Blackie. And he caught the hand of Andy Connell.

Andy Connell brushed him away.

'I always told you,' cried Mrs Connell; 'I always told you that Blackie would come out on top! I always told you that Red was a snake.

237

I hope you'll listen to me once in a while after this. Poor Blackie, he's all broke up over the thing!'

Blackie had sunk into a chair and dropped his face in both his hands, as though, indeed, the consummate wickedness of his foster brother was more than he could endure.

'You got nothing else to say, then?' cried Andy Connell.

And Red could only be silent, wondering how God permitted such wrong on the wretched earth.

He finished his musing very briefly. 'I got nothing to say,' he admitted.

'Get out of the house—out of my sight. And God forgive me for havin' raised up a snake in the place of a man.'

So Red, with one wild glance around him, ran stumbling through the doorway and, still stumbling, across the open toward the barn; and behind him, from the door, the wild, broken voice of Andy Connell followed him with curses.

It was the end of the world, the downfall of all right, the kingdom of wrong!

CHAPTER THIRTY

RED STICKS

He would take with him, he determined, only those things which were his of his own right and not the gift of Andy Connell. So he hurried first to the shed where he had left his rifle and revolver, after Joe Hooker's last lesson in marksmanship of that morning. There he belted them on. Then he went to the barn and took the saddle which he had won at the bucking contest two summers before. So he continued to the corral where Spitfire remained by herself, and the bright-eyed mare came up to him uncalled, unpersuaded, and began to sniff at the burden of leather and of iron which he carried.

Yes, she stood even without a rope on her neck while he placed that saddle on her back.

'It's my luck!' said Red gloomily to himself. 'When I've lost everything else, the horse comes to me. God bless her.'

When she felt the bite of the cinches, she snapped her head around and laid hold on his arm; but at the first word she relaxed her grip. So he completed the saddling and raised himself gently and settled in the saddle. She went off at a gentle trot with pricking ears like the best trained saddle horse in the world.

Indeed, it seemed like a stroke of fate that she should have become so suddenly manageable. She went off through the hills with her head in the air and her gait as light as blown foam across the trails. The sullen pain in the heart of Red began to lessen, and it seemed to him, after all, that this was the life for which he was intended—a lonely life, unshielded by friends or money from the country itself, with one or two bosom companions—like Joe Hooker.

And as for work, why not begin as a cowpuncher, and then work, perhaps, into an interest in some small ranch, and all that he owned have as the product of the work of his own hands, while Blackie reveled in the unearned millions which he would inherit from old Andy Connell. It was a prospect which satisfied Red Hardwick, and as he rode, he wondered that such a solution had never come into his mind before. He had looked forward to the inheritance from Andy Connell as a necessary thing—a thing without which he could hardly live. Now that the blow had fallen, he felt that he was above being affected by it. The concern of it was all removed from him.

So thought Red Hardwick as he sent Spitfire spinning along the crest of a narrow ridge, and then flew her down the easy slope beyond. He had worked, gradually, up into the mountains, and now he headed instinctively toward a place where he and Joe Hooker had often ridden.

It was a dry valley several miles in length, with steep walls on either side, but these walls were carved away on both hands by narrow ravines. There were three ravines on either side, running at a leisurely angle up from the floor of the valley. Joe Hooker had often pointed out that valley as a place where a man should ride if he were pursued by numbers.

'Because,' Joe had said, 'the whole floor of the valley is covered with flint so hard that it won't show the dent of a horse's hoof, and once you get into the valley you can ride straight through it—it's the easiest way through the heart of the hills—or else you can turn to one side or the other, three chances on side and three chances on the other. Why, man, you got seven things to do, and the boys after you would have seven things to think about!'

They had often ridden into the valley and taken cognizance of its possibilities. And now Red Hardwick let his mare saunter gently toward the place—gently, until he saw over the rim of a western hill the shadow of a flying horseman printed for an instant against the sky and then dipping down the nearer slope. He did not need to look twice. Even at that distance, he knew the splendid gray of Joe Hooker, and the singular seat of Joe Hooker in the saddle, with a way of twisting his right shoulder far forward, riding slanting. He loosed the reins of Spitfire and she flew on toward the mouth of the black valley. A shout and a wave of the hand made the approaching rider take note of him, and as he took note, a gun winked into the hand of Hooker.

It told Red what from the speed of the horse and the desperate earnestness of the rider, he had been able to guess that Joe Hooker had at last 'kicked over the traces' and now he was flying for his life.

At the very entrance of the valley their horses met, and Red shouted:

'What's up, Joe?'

'Hell fire!' answered Joe, and waved behind him.

They were already in view. Over the crest of the hill where Hooker had ridden, a half dozen riders came pouring, and now, at a distance behind, still others. Hooker and Red pushed their own horses into the mouth of the valley and out of sight.

'Take my horse, Joe,' begged Red. 'Take my horse. I'll tell them that you held me up and made me give it to you.'

'I'll live or die with the gray,' answered Hooker tersely.

'But with you *on* the gray, Joe, what's let them keep so close?'

'When they got to Mooney's, they found that he had his horses all bunched in his corrals, ready for a try at selling them. They hopped into those corrals and picked out the best of the lot, and you know that Mooney has some good nags. So they've got fresh horseflesh under them and they're driving me into the ground.'

'Joe, which way'll you turn?'

'This way, maybe!' snarled out Joe savagely, and he swung about in his saddle and stared behind him, his rifle held at the ready.

He continued: 'You get out of this, kid. This is my own little job. Vamoose!'

'I'll stick with you, Joe,' said Red with emotion, 'until you sink a bullet in me. But don't use the rifle, Joe. Don't use it until they have you cornered. What in the world has happened?'

'A fool came along begging me to kill him. And at last I done it.'

'Who?'

'Young Larry Rawson.'

'The devil! He's a fine fellow, Joe.'

'He was fine, maybe. But he ain't now. I never done a thing that I hated worse. But the fool kid drove me back and drove me back. I'd of had to take water before all of Jackson Corners to keep away from a fight with him. Here!'

As he spoke, he swung the gray—which was now almost black with running sweat—into the throat of a gully.

'Wrong, wrong!' cried out Red. 'They expect you to head south toward the border. Take the other side of the valley and ride north—'

'You're right, kid. By the heavens, you're

243

right!'

And Joe Hooker swung the gray squarely about and spurred it cruelly across the volcanic floor of the valley and into the mouth of a ravine on the opposite side. Red Hardwick, flying half a stride behind him, thought that he saw the head of the pursuit come into view at the same moment, but he could not be sure.

In another instant they had turned around the first shoulder of the twisting ravine and were again lost from the sight of the pursuers. Here Joe Hooker flung himself from his horse and led it forward. He commanded Red to do the same thing.

'Because if they hear us,' said Hooker, 'it's the same as if they saw us—and a horse makes twice as much noise with its feet with a man on its back.'

Out of the main floor of the valley behind them they heard a turmoil of shouting, all the voices sounding dreamlike in the distance, but they went plodding steadily on, looking at each other with big eyes, now and then, but saying nothing, as if merely a whisper might betray them. And then, right behind them, filling the narrow pass with thunder, they heard the roar of the hoofs of galloping horses.

'They've found us, Joe!' cried Red. And he caught his mare by the bridle, preparatory to swinging onto her back.

The lean hand of Joe Hooker caught and held him.

'Maybe they've found our trail—maybe they ain't. Maybe they're just doing a little exploring. Wait and see.'

He turned and rested the rifle in the crook of his arm. Up the ravine, the noise of the pursuit washed like a great wave that crowds a shoaling beach with thunder and pushes far up a rocky inlet. It stormed almost upon them and then paused. There was only a single elbow bend of the ravine between them and the danger.

'I'll be darned,' said one, 'if I go another step. We're killing our horses running up mountainsides; and the sheriff ought to have better sense. Besides, Hooker ain't here. He rode right straight through the valley. I think I had a peek at him as he turned out at the end of the valley.'

'He wasn't that far ahead; he couldn't have got to the end of the valley before we seen him.'

'He has a fast hoss under him.'

'But his hoss is spent. Let's go a ways farther up this draw—'

'Not a step. I'm not going to kill my hoss for the sheriff.'

'Stay where you are, then. Come on, boys. We'll have a look at—'

'He ain't up this way,' answered another voice. 'There ain't no sign—'

'He wouldn't leave none on rock as hard as this here.'

'I'm through. Come on back, Billy. Unless

you want to try him by yourself.'

There was a protesting oath from Billy; then the sound of the horses receded. And Red drew a long breath as he saw the ready rifle dropped from the arm of Joe Hooker.

'That,' said Joe, 'is the closest I ever come to killing, and if I'd had to shoot—'

'Whether you drove them back or not, it would have been the end of you.'

'Unless I could have gotten clean out of the country,' admitted Hooker. 'This Guernsey is a bulldog. He's gunna give me trouble. And now, Red, you nearly got in the same hornet's nest with me. Hit the back trail, kid!'

'Not in a thousand years,' said Red.

CHAPTER THIRTY-ONE

PURSUIT

They drifted over the crest of the hills slowly, making north. And still Joe Hooker walked at the side of his gray horse, with the cinches loosened.

'Suppose that they rush you—the whole gang of them?' suggested Red anxiously.

'Look at Jim,' said Hooker. 'Look at Jim Dandy. He ain't blowing his head off any more. He ain't trailin' his feet. He's pickin' his head up a mite. Well, old son, if they do sight me and rush me, I don't mind tellin' you that I'll have time to hop into the saddle and then jest blow away from 'em, son. They've give me a bad time with their fresh hosses. But now I'm ready to run with the best of 'em. Another fifteen minutes and Jim will be all blowed out and about as good as ever. But boy, boy, how they come hoppin' over the hills after me. I thought that I'd never see that old valley, and if I did, I thought that they'd be so close onto my heels that I wouldn't have a chance to dodge and hide. It was a sort of a jumpy time. But you, Red, what the devil brings you out here, makin' a fool of yourself hangin' around with a man-killer like me?'

To him, Red told the story of his loss of a home, told it all as briefly as it could be crammed into terse words.

'Only,' said Joe Hooker, 'I want to know if what you said was the truth. *Did* you go around and raise that money for a friend?'

'On my word.'

'What friend?'

'Blackie.'

Joe Hooker gasped. 'You really mean it, Red? You really mean that you *did* give that money to the sneaking, double-tongued, poison-carryin' son of a gun, Blackie?'

'I did,' said Red.

'Then,' said Joe Hooker, after a moment of profane comment, 'you deserve everything that's coming to you!'

'I do,' said Red, 'and I know it. Look, Joe, they're coming!'

Sheriff Sid Guernsey had started every man of his lot cutting around the valley to find sign of the fugitive, and now the sign had been found and the whole posse came humming over the hills after the gun fighter. But Joe Hooker's prophecy was more than borne out. He had time to draw the cinches tight, swing into the saddle, and when the gray horse started away, it was with a light and easy stride that dropped the posse far and farther behind every instant.

In a scant hour the pursuit had disappeared from the horizon. There, in a rocky tract between two hills, Joe Hooker paused to construct a trail puzzle that would have troubled the keen wits of a grizzly bear. Then he went on again, and Red with him, into the yellow light of the end of the day, with the sun hanging low on their left hand.

The sun had turned crimson and squatted on top of a western peak when they came in sight of a solitary man moving before them down the heart of a shallow valley. He was not walking, but striking out at a steady dog trot.

'A Mexican,' said Joe Hooker at once. 'And a Mexican will do me no harm. He may give me news that I want to know.'

So they freshened the pace of their horses and hurried on at a round canter. When the pedestrian, however, heard the sound of the hoofs behind him, he turned, and then started off like a rabbit toward the nearest brush. He was far too late for an escape, however.

'He's been up to some deviltry,' shouted Joe to Red. 'That makes him meat for us.'

When they came closer, the other suddenly whirled and flung himself flat along the ground, with a rifle pitched into the hollow of his shoulder.

'Pull up, Red!' shouted Hooker. 'Pull up, or the fool will do us some harm.'

He set the example, and at the same time raised his right hand high above his head in token of amity.

A sharp voice cautioned them: 'Who are you, amigos? Why have you followed me?'

'I always follow a man that runs,' answered Joe Hooker. 'I'm Joe Hooker; does that mean anything to you? I'm not the sheriff, and I'm not one of the sheriff's men. Does that mean anything more?'

The Mexican arose, still with his rifle ready. 'Señor,' said he, 'my horse has broken his leg in a prairie dog's hole. Never before have I needed a friend so greatly. If you will help me, señor, God will bless you, and I have fifteen dollars to pay you for your trouble.'

'This poor devil,' said Hooker aside to Red, 'is in the same boat with me.' He added, aloud, as he let his gray horse work nearer: 'What trouble have you dropped into, amigo?'

'I?' said the Mexican. 'I, señor, am in no

trouble at all, if you please.'

Joe Hooker merely grinned at him. 'Let's tell the truth to one another,' said he, 'because we may need one another before we're through with the next day. You have no horse; we have two horses, and if you prove yourself of the right stuff, you take it with my word that we will not leave you in the lurch. I will begin. I'm Joe Hooker, and the reason I'm spending the night in the hills instead of in Jackson Corners is because there is a dead man in that town, and the sheriff wants me.'

The Mexican started violently and turned not white, because the color of his skin forbade such a change, but a dingy yellow.

'You, too, señor?' he could not help exclaiming.

'The devil!' exclaimed Hooker. 'Have you done the same thing?'

'No—' began the Mexican, and then changed his mind in mid speech. 'Señor, I shall trust you. There is indeed a dead man behind me. I have killed Lew Bender by the hotel.'

'This,' said Joe Hooker, 'is getting sort of wonderful. That was the gun shot that made poor Larry Rawson jump pretty nigh out of his skin, and then like a young fool pull his gun on me. So you're the bird that was in the trees doing the shooting?'

'There were two shots, señor!' cried the Mexican. 'I stood before him face to face. It was fair fight. Only by so much'—and he held

250

up his hand, pinching thumb and forefinger close together—'only by so much my bullet arrived first and his bullet twitched aside and lifted the hair by my forehead.'

He paused and added solemnly: 'I swear to the high God, señor, that it was done in the fairest fight. I could not fight my own brother more fairly. Besides, I had a great command to kill him. I tell you, señor, that a man as good as an angel from heaven came to me and told me to kill him. Otherwise, what profit was it to me? Did I rob him? I did not. I did not take so much as the gun which had dropped from his hand. But as he fell, so I left him. I swear it, señor!'

'This is all the truth, amigo,' answered Joe Hooker gently. 'Very well. Here we are, the pair of us, having dropped our men. The sheriff is after me; he will be after you, too, in time. And so we'll team it, eh?'

'Alas, Señor Hooker, I have no horse.'

'We'll make the first march without a horse and trust to God to get us a nag to-morrow to fit you out. What is your name?'

'My name is José Ridal.'

'Ridal, we know one another.' He held out his hand and closed it upon the hand of the Mexican. Then Red Hardwick was called up and introduced.

'This,' said Hooker, 'is an old friend who has lost his home, and he has thrown in his luck with mine—like a fool kid!'

José Ridal acknowledged the introduction

with a broad grin. 'Only,' said he, 'I cannot tell why you will choose to help a man not known to you, like myself, señor!'

'Listen to me,' answered Joe Hooker, while Red listened with a peculiar interest. 'I've been around the world, and now when I see a man that I can cotton to, I know his face right off. The way that I know yours, José. You'd never down a pal or knife a friend. I could trust you, José.'

José smiled. 'This is all very well,' said he. 'Now, my friend, help me to-day and you will find that I shall be able to help you to-morrow.'

So they struck off up the valley, and it was some time before Red Hardwick had a chance to speak with Joe Hooker apart. Then he said: 'Why do you do it, Joe? If Guernsey gets on your trail again, as he's apt to, we're all lost, because one horse will have to carry double!'

'I don't know,' admitted Joe Hooker. 'But when I saw the poor devil stumbling along on foot, my heart went out to him, and I follow my heart, Red. It's the only way that I know how to live and be happy, no matter what comes.'

It seemed a sufficiently mysterious thing to Red, but he made no answer.

They kept on well into the dark, until the limping of the Mexican forced them to make a halt. He was footsore from his labors of that day, and while he washed and bound up his feet in rags at a little brook that they met, the other two made the camp and cut down young boughs of pine and fir to make the three beds. They did not risk a fire, of course. And there was no food. But all three had gone hungry before this day. So they drew up their belts another notch, smoked a final cigarette—for a goodnight smoke is the cure of all evils—and then rolled into their fragrant beds. And, in an instant, they were sound asleep.

Or at least, they were lost in sleep as sound as that which ever comes to hunted men. Midnight passed, and the sky was already gray when Joe Hooker sat up and hissed softly; and the other two as they opened their eyes heard him say:

'We have the luck of the devil himself. They are coming, pals! They must have camped higher up on this same brook.'

CHAPTER THIRTY-TWO

CORNERED

Twice, as they flung the saddles on the horses, the eyes of José Ridal darted askance at the shrubbery near by, as though he considered finding shelter there. But each glance must have made him see the folly of such a hope. For it was a ghost of a shelter. It made hardly more than a thin mist on the hillside, and a man's body could not be sheltered there from the most casual glance.

He turned his attention with a redoubled interest to the saddling of the horses, which was completed in jig time. Then the three started down the hillside, the horses walking, even though the riders were hungry for speed—walking while the noise of the man hunters grew louder and bolder behind them every moment.

As they worked over the sandy ground beside the brook, Joe Hooker said: 'If we can get out of sight, they ain't so apt to foller our trail. They know that I got one more man with me, and they'll be looking for the trail of two horses, not for two horses and a man on foot beside 'em.'

They were never to know what held the posse such an unconscionable time behind the heads of the hills, but at any rate, they were able presently to turn unseen into the shallow hiding of the next hollow. Here José Ridal was taken up on the stirrup and then behind the cantle of Joe Hooker's saddle, and the horses broke away, but not at a burning gallop.

'We need their wind; we need their wind!' called Hooker after Red Hardwick. 'Let 'em take it easy.'

So they dropped to a sharp trot, Jim Dandy flattening his ears at the double labor which he was compelled to do.

And they had covered much ground when, behind them, they heard a far-off single shout, followed by an outcry like the opening of a pack of hounds.

'They've got more sense than I thought,' declared Joe Hooker. 'They figger that this *is* our trail. And here they come. Step up, Jim Dandy. Come along, boy!'

Jim Dandy answered with a valiant effort and they spun down the hollow at a round gallop, with the valiant gray seeming to run as lightly as though he had not more than four hundred pounds of man and saddle on his back. When Red offered to take the Mexican on his horse in turn, Joe Hooker shook his head.

'I ain't done my share yet,' said he.

They came to the course of a shallow little stream twisting among the hills like a writhing snake.

'Angle your hoss downstream,' said Joe to Red, and started the gray in as though he intended to follow down the current. Instead, he wheeled the gray in the narrow sweep of water and began to rush him up the water. Red followed as a matter of course.

There was hardly more than a foot of water; the current was not fast, and the bed of the stream was well compacted, heavy gravel, so that even Jim Dandy, with his double load could trot through the stream. Now, behind them, the rapid muttering of the hoofs of galloping horses came nearer, and Red, as the rear guard, unlimbered his rifle.

It is a hard thing to say of Red, but the truth is that had the best and the most law-abiding man in the county appeared at that moment on the trail, he would have tried a fair shot at the worthy with hardly more compunction than he would have used in drawing a bead at a tree squirrel. Following the course of the water, they had twisted out of sight of the floor of the hollow before one of the pursuit appeared. Joe Hooker then consented that Red should take José Ridal up behind the cantle of the mare, and they rode out of the stream and cantered down its farther bank.

Spitfire at first was inclined to pitch at this new incubus which had been placed upon her back, but she settled down almost at once, so much difference had a single day of hard riding made in her training. She submitted to voice and hand and went along smoothly enough, and more strongly than even Jim Dandy.

'You see,' said Joe Hooker, watching her action with an eye of admiration, 'what a difference it makes when they're allowed to grow up free—and wild? She'd be a spindly thing if she'd been caught up and worked from her third year.'

But, in the meantime, the voice of the Mexican was at the ear of Red Hardwick.

'Señor, it is I who will carry you both to your deaths. I am not worthy. See, *amigo mio*, there are many crimes behind me. I am not worthy that two good men should risk themselves for me. Let me jump down. I shall run up that hillside and try to hide among the rocks.'

'There are no rocks there big enough to hide a chipmunk,' said Red calmly. 'Stay with us, Ridal. Have we complained of you yet?'

There was a devout burst of Spanish from the lips of José Ridal, and Red knew that the fellow was offering up a prayer to his special saint for the sake of the two 'gringos' who had rescued him.

They put such a stretch of ground behind them, before poor Sheriff Guernsey was able to decipher the simple little trail puzzle, that they did not see the sheriff's men again that day—the second of the pursuit. That night they came to a ranch house in the hills—a tumble-down shack inhabited by an old man and his son.

'Look here,' said Joe Hooker, as he appeared at the door, 'I'm Joe Hooker; d'you know me?'

The old man merely winced, but his son resolutely reached for a rifle which hung on the wall. He got his hand to it, but he also found the steady revolver of Joe Hooker looking him in the eye, so his arm fell to his side again.

'You've got a good-looking brown gelding in the corral,' said Joe. 'What's the price of it?'

'That's a seventy-five-dollar hoss,' said the old rancher.

'It's too high a price,' said Joe Hooker, 'because that's just a mustang. But I'm gunna give you a hundred. The extra change will buy

257

us a meal from you. Eh?'

At this the old chap squinted sharply at him. 'Are you gunna have me set down as the hired man of a crook and a man-killer?' he asked. 'It ain't in me, Hooker—no matter what you and your two pals may do to me and me boy.'

'Who would know,' said Hooker, 'that we gave you any hire? You can tell them that we robbed you of a hoss and that we stuck you up and made you cook us a meal.'

'That ain't so bad,' admitted the veteran. 'Come in and rest your feet, boys. I'll have you a snack fixed up in a jiffy. Tom, go out and fetch in the brown. Maybe you'd want a saddle for that hoss?'

'We would.'

'Throw Josh Curry's saddle on the brown.'

'How much will that cost us?'

'Nothin'! I'm makin' enough money off you the way it is. Josh is dead, you see. And his saddle by rights is dead, too. But it's a place to set in, and it's got stirrups for your feet. It's better'n nothin'. Hop along, Tom!'

'Shall I go with him?' whispered Red to Joe.

'Not a step,' answered Joe from the corner of his mouth. 'These fellers are white, and they know the right white-man's ways. They won't double cross us.'

There they ate of the best that the house could provide. The money was counted into the hand of the old cattleman. Tom brought in the brown gelding, and they departed with a ring of good wishes behind them.

The third day they crossed the divide of the range and dropped onto the northeastern side; they rose for the fourth morning with a feeling that safety was certainly in their grasp at last and found that Ridal's brown gelding had gone lame.

The Mexican turned gray. 'The first,' said he, 'was bad luck, but when a man is struck down twice, what shall I call it? It is the hand of God, my friends. And I am no better than a dead man, for they shall never take me alive.'

'You talk like a fool!' Joe Hooker told him bluntly. 'Walk the gelding around a little. He's only cold and stiff.'

But exercise made no difference. The gelding was hopelessly gone. They left him to graze as he would, and they started on again as they had done in the first place, with the two on horseback, and José Ridal striding at the side. But all the heart was gone from him now.

'They will find us; they will find us,' he repeated. 'God has spoken against us, friends, and there is no escape—leave José Ridal behind you, for there is a curse on him!'

They paid no attention to those lamentations, however, but in the late evening of the fourth day, as they looked about them for a proper place to camp and started toward the mouth of a narrow, wooded ravine, José Ridal stumbled and fell, and before he struck

259

the ground, the clangor of rifles was in the ears of the two riders.

Many a time Red Hardwick had leaned from his saddle and scooped the handkerchief from the ground. He leaned now, without changing the stride of his trotting horse, and scooped up the Mexican. Hot blood spurted across his hand and his arm as he did so. But he brought Ridal safely across the pommel of his saddle. A deep groan from José gave promise that the Mexican was not yet dead, and with Hooker ahead, showing the way, they raced up the slope of the hill on their left.

They hardly had reached its crest, where a little deserted shack stood, a tumble-down tiny ruin, than a crackle of guns rose from the valley beyond, and they saw half a dozen horsemen rushing up toward them.

There was nothing else to be done; they whirled back to the shack. José was dragged inside it, and Joe Hooker, with a shout and a wave of his arms, frightened their horses away down the opposite slope.

'Because,' said he, 'it's a lot better that the sheriff should have 'em than that they should get filled full of lead.'

There was no danger of a charge. On all sides they heard the jubilant shouting of the posse, and, afterward, they could hear the sharp voice of the sheriff giving his orders.

'He's got forty men with him. He's travelin' with a whole army,' said Joe Hooker sadly.

'Here,' said Red. 'Look at José!'

There was no need of even such skill as Joe possessed. It was too plain that José was a dying man.

CHAPTER THIRTY-THREE

NEAR DEATH

But through that night, Ridal refused to die. He clung stubbornly to his life. They had made a little torch of pine wood and screened it so that the light fell upon Ridal. But still it gave no advantage to those who watched without and who, from time to time, pumped a rifle bullet through the shack by way of keeping the inhabitants awake, one might have said.

'There are two agonies upon me, friends,' said José faintly. 'The first is that I have brought you to such an end because I am cursed. And the next is that I must die by candlelight. Who knows,' he added, with a break of feverish superstition and a wild rolling of his eyes, 'who knows if I might not find the way to heaven under the light of the sun. But this candlelight—'

The pine torch was flaring high, and the flood of yellow light was falling directly upon the face of José, but so dulled were his eyes that he seemed to see only a glimmer.

261

They had made the big bandage around his body as well as they were able; but still the blood speeded through the cloth.

'Do you see?' said José to them faintly. 'Life is a well of water, but mine is broken, and the water is running out swiftly!'

Red Hardwick could endure no more. He jumped up and left the cabin and, from the brink in the hill, he looked down. It was a pleasant picture, that picture of the outer night.

Sheriff Guernsey had ringed the hill on which the cabin stood with little camp fires—a dozen, perhaps, in all. They cast a light from one point of the circle to the next and threw long, tossing shadows up the slope. In the rocks behind the fire, securely fortified as in so many nests, were the men of the posse, two or more to every fire, with rifles constantly leveled and revolvers always at hand.

Sheriff Guernsey would not allow sleepiness to overcome his men. He ordered that at each fire one man should be resting—sleeping if he could. The other man or men were to keep awake and watch. And, in order to make sure that the watchfulness should not lag, he had ordered three men to be constantly crawling about from post to post, with brandy and food. When the morning came, it would be a simple thing to riddle that wretched little shack with rifle fire and drive out or kill the fugitives. The game was entirely in his hand, and the sheriff knew it. So did Red, as he lay on his belly on the cold hillside and studied the scene.

He called loudly: 'Guernsey! Sid Guernsey.'

A rifle spoke in answer, and the bullet ripped up the ground before him and cast a shower of sand into his face.

'Stop that shooting!' barked the shrill voice of Guernsey.

'My finger done it, not me,' said the guilty man.

'What do you want?' called Guernsey.

'I want to come down and talk to you.'

'Come down, then,' said Guernsey. 'You'll go back safe enough, but stop in front of the fires. Don't try to break through the line. You'll be covered.'

Red went down and stood exactly in front of the fires. A shadow among shadows, Guernsey arose from the rocks beyond.

'Well, Red,' he said, 'you've got yourself into good company, and you been givin' comfort and help to them that the law wants. I dunno how many years in jail you'll get, even if you give yourself up now. I suppose that's what you come down for?'

'You suppose wrong. We got a dying man up in the shack.'

'Hooker?'

'No, Ridal.'

'The devil; what's he to me?'

'Nothing, I suppose. Is there a doctor in the lot of you?'

263

'Speak up, boys,' called Guernsey. 'Is there a doctor among us? No,' he added after pausing a moment for a reply, 'there ain't. But what d'you want?'

'Somebody who can make the Mexican comfortable while he dies. There's not much hope for him.'

Guernsey paused again. 'It would be a fool thing for me to come myself. But I got a doctoring kit, and—Red, I'll come.'

There was a chorus of protest from the posse—warnings that Guernsey would be taken and held for their own safety by the fugitives if he went up to the cabin; but Guernsey scoffed their warnings aside.

'I know Hooker better than that,' said he. 'And I know Red. They ain't rats.'

And up the hill he went at the side of Red Hardwick.

They found José Ridal fallen into a weak calm, his face haggard and his eyes closed and sunken. Joe Hooker, at the side of the dying man, acknowledged the presence of the sheriff by a nod only. And Guernsey set about examining the wound. He shook his head at once, drew out a brandy flask, and gave Ridal a stiff draw.

'There ain't nothing that can be done,' said he. 'He's drifting out fast.'

Under the stimulus, Ridal opened his wild eyes and looked vaguely at them.

'Who is this?' said he huskily to Guernsey.

'Is it not my father's cousin? Are you not Pedro Gonzales, the priest?'

'I am,' said Guernsey calmly.

'That is good,' sighed Ridal. 'As for my own soul, it is lost and can never be saved, father. But my two friends—this Señor Hardwick and this Señor Hooker, have risked their lives for my life. Do you hear me, father? Pray for them. Pray them into heaven.'

'Well,' muttered Guernsey, 'what is your own crime, José?' he asked in good Spanish.

'I killed a man like a rat; his name is Bender, but that is not all.'

'Did you kill him for his money, José?'

'I did not touch his purse,' said the dying man. 'I killed him for the sake of a friend. A friend asked me to take him out of his way, and I killed him. Before this man, this Bender fought with me, I heard him tell the truth. He had come to get much money out of Señor Lewis Connell.'

'Ah?' said the sheriff.

'Because of that, Señor Connell wished him dead, and I killed him, father. But that is not the sin which damns me—that is—' His eyes roved eagerly. 'Is that light beyond the windows the sunrise, father?' He pointed to the flickering lights from the camp fires which showed against the panes of glass.

'It's the sunrise,' answered Joe Hooker, understanding.

'I thank God,' said José Ridal. 'I could not

265

die in the dark of the night. Amigo—' said he to Joe Hooker, and as he laid his hand on the arm of the cow-puncher, he stiffened, choked, and looked up to the roof with sightless eyes. He was dead.

The sheriff himself closed those horrible, open eyes and laid a blanket over the form of the dead man. Then he said to Red: 'What is this stuff about Blackie?'

'I don't know,' said Red.

'However,' said the sheriff, 'it'll bear looking into. Red, I ask you now for the last time: D'you stick here with Joe until the fighting starts, or do you come along with me?'

'You go along with him,' insisted Hooker.

'I stick here, and that's final,' said Red.

'Red,' began Hooker, 'if you—'

'Persuading,' said the sheriff, 'will do no good. He's set in his mind.'

And he left the cabin unhindered and went down the slope to the circle of fires. There, as he sat huddled inside a blanket he was heard to say: 'Did you ever set a trap for a skunk and get a lion?'

But after that he did not speak again until the night was old and the gray of the dawn began, first as a chill stir in the air, and then a sudden blackening of the eastern mountains, so that they seemed to swallow half the sky, and finally a thin rim of gray along the tops of the peaks. Still it was not time to begin the shooting which must finish Hooker and his companion. And even when the sky had turned to rose, the sheriff was not yet ready.

It was at this time that some one announced a horseman headed toward them and they saw a rider hurrying a tired horse over the last hill. It was a young puncher from a neighboring town, his horse covered with lather.

'Is Guernsey here?' he asked.

'I'm Guernsey,' said the sheriff.

The messenger slipped from his horse. 'I see,' he nodded, 'and Hooker is up yonder, trapped?'

'He is,' grinned the sheriff.

'Well,' said the other, 'open the trap and let him out. You've done a lot of riding for nothing.'

'Riding for nothing?' shouted Sid Guernsey.

'Larry Rawson is alive,' explained the other.

There was a muttering exclamation from the crowd.

'The telegraph was chattering last night,' said the messenger. 'When they found that you'd passed through the town yesterday, they burned up the wire telling us that Rawson is alive and that he's sure to get well, and that he ain't pressing no charges against Hooker. He says that it was a fair fight, and that he started the fighting. Hooker shot in self-defense!'

The sheriff stood like one stunned. And then he struck a hand against his face.

'Now,' said he, 'I got something to thank God for, which is something I thought that

Hooker would never give me. Go call him down; he's come within an ace of bein' a dead man.'

CHAPTER THIRTY-FOUR

RED'S INHERITANCE

Mrs Connell had become Blackie's chief adviser. And when he pointed out to her that Andy seemed less fond of him than ever, since Red had been driven out of the house, she simply said: 'Keep away from him, Blackie. He was always wrapped up in Red, and because he's done justice on him and drove him out of the house, that don't mean that he likes you any better than ever. He's got a lot of things agin' you. But keep quiet and don't let him hear you chirping none because Red is down and you're up. Only tell me, Blackie—was it for you that Red borrowed the money?'

'Certainly not,' said Blackie. But he smiled at her, and she understood.

Andy Connell, indeed, was like a man who had lost his very soul. He roamed through the house and over his place; he went to the mine and probed foolishly among its nooks and corners as though he were hunting for a dear possession which was gone from him. To his wife he uttered only monosyllables; to Blackie he did not speak at all.

'He'll even things up,' declared Blackie, 'by leaving most of his money to some charity.'

'No,' said Mrs Connell. 'Keep your mouth shut and don't bother him none and he'll never take the trouble to look for a charity. It'll all come to you. And then—'

'Oh,' said he, 'I won't forget you, Mrs Connell.'

'That,' said she grimly, 'is something that you'd better not.'

It was on the seventh day after the departure of Red in disgrace that there appeared at the house of Andy Connell the two most distinguished visitors he had ever received—none other than Chalmer Greenough from Yates Valley, and his daughter Beatrice.

Even rough Andy was stirred. He took them up to the mine and showed them where the gold was first struck—first found in a broken stone in the meadow land below; then followed to an obscure outcropping on the side of the hill above, and how the vein had opened out as they followed it through the hill to the other side. Mr Greenough was charmed. He had made his own millions and many of them, but he had never made them so simply as this. He went through the mine from top to bottom, and he found a time to take Connell apart and say: 'Connell, I suppose that you've heard Blackie speak of my daughter?'

'I have,' said the miner.

269

'And I,' said Greenough, 'have heard her talk of Lewis. In one word, my friend, I've come over here to-day to let you understand that if those young people are really fond of one another, I shall not stand in their way.'

'You won't?' gasped out Connell. 'Why, sir, if Blackie is gunna be as lucky as that, I don't mind tellin' you that he's the single heir to all that I've got.'

'That,' said Greenough with much satisfaction, 'is very much to the point. Not, you understand, that Beatrice has spoken to me definitely. But I can see that she inclines to Lewis. From the day when he kept her and her horse from a nasty accident in Jackson Corners, she had always felt that there was something owing to him.'

So Andy Connell walked the air as they strolled back down the hill, with Blackie and Beatrice before them, laughing together.

They were almost at the bottom of the hill when she pointed and cried out: 'Isn't that Red, coming toward us?'

'Hush!' cautioned Blackie. 'That's a name Mr Connell doesn't want to hear; besides, it can't be Red. He's been driven out.'

But it *was* Red, and on either side of him rode on the one hand the sheriff, and on the other hand tall Joe Hooker; and they came straight for the astonished Andy Connell.

'Lemme talk!' said Andy. 'If the sheriff has brung them two in for some sort of crooked

270

work, I'll tell him pretty pronto that I ain't behind young Hardwick.'

He strode out before the rest, with an ominous face. But he was not the goal in the eye of Sheriff Sid Guernsey. That warrior of the mountain desert rode briskly past Connell with only a wave of the hand, touched the brim of his hat to Beatrice, nodded to Mr Greenough, and brought his horse to a halt in front of Blackie.

'Good morning, sheriff,' said Blackie as pleasantly as he could.

The answer of the sheriff was simply: 'Young feller, what d'you know of the killing of Lew Bender?'

When one has crossed a frightful chasm and stands safely on the other side, it is bewildering to find the same gulf under one's eyes again. Blackie, for all the steadiness of his nerves, was shaken to the ground, and from his lips burst the telltale exclamation: 'My God!'

That, and the sudden whiteness of his face was proof enough. But the sheriff thrust out a gloved hand and held Blackie while he stabbed the next question at him.

'Bender came here to collect gambling debts from you, Blackie. Is that right?'

Andy Connell at that instant turned squarely upon Blackie. And on either side of him was the lady of his heart—his hope of millions—and her shrewd father. The frightful consequences that might ensue if he were to

271

stumble, choked Blackie. Another instant, and he could have lied smoothly and with an unchanging face. But now this combination of dangers closed his throat and put a pound of lead upon his tongue. He could not speak.

'And when he come to you for the money, you was afraid to ask Connell, there, for it. And you went to Red, there, for help, and Red helped you. And then when he'd raised the money for you—'

'Ten thousand damnations!' shouted Andy Connell. 'It ain't no ways possible!' And he rushed at Blackie and caught him by the shoulders.

'Blackie, after he risked himself for the sake of savin' you—him—Red—after the way you always treated him—and then to turn around and knife him—but—my head is turnin' upside down. It ain't possible!'

'It's all a lie!' said Blackie through his poor, numb lips.

But oh, what a weak voice it was, and how falteringly it issued from his lips.

'Let's go away!' said Beatrice Greenough to her father, sick at what she saw.

'No!' said he sternly. 'We'll stay here and see this thing out. I think we may be attending the unveiling of a rare rogue, Beatrice. It will be worth seeing.'

What little self-possession had remained to Blackie melted away under this stroke from the side. He strove to rally; he thought of flight, and he winced in the hands of Andy Connell. The rough miner wanted no more. He flung Blackie away and the latter, stumbling, fell flat upon the ground.

When he stood up, every back was toward him except the long, lean face of Joe Hooker, wreathed in a sinister grin of satisfaction. And the cow-puncher hooked his thumb over his shoulder and down the road as if to say: 'That's the way for you to take, kid. Run along!'

That was not the chief agony for Blackie, however. It did not seem possible that in so few seconds all the ground could be ripped away from under his feet. And here was the sheriff saying:

'You're under arrest, young Connell. Take him out to the barn, Joe, and get him on a hoss. I'll trust him to you. We're gunna see if killings can be bought and paid for in this here land while I'm the sheriff of it.'

So Blackie was led away, and as he went he saw Andy Connell put his thick arm around the shoulders of Red and heard him crying: 'Red, by the Eternal, you've been brung back to me. This'll turn Rica green, I tell you. It'll turn her green, but it's warmth in my heart! After this, I'll never grow old. Only, Red, how are you gunna learn how to forgive me for the fool that I've been in treatin' you this way?'

'Why,' Blackie heard Red say, 'I'm glad it all happened. Because from this time on, I guess it will take a good deal to break in between us, eh?'

'There ain't enough dynamite in the world to blast us apart,' declared the other with a ringing oath.

Was not that enough for Blackie to see and to hear? No, there was still more agony for him, the keenest touch of all. He saw Chalmer Greenough lay a hand upon the shoulder of Red and say: 'I know all about this old enmity between you and Blackie, and if you've tried to do such a thing for him at the end of all your rivalry—why, it was a very fine thing, young man!'

Blackie waited to hear no more. Not even from Beatrice, was a single pitying glance sent after him, and he hurried away at the side of Joe Hooker.

'Oh, God!' cried Blackie suddenly. 'I wish that I was dead!'

'I'll loan you a gun for the job,' said Joe Hooker without mercy. 'Eat rat poison, son, and die the kind of a death that you're intended for.'

*   *   *

They did not throw Blackie into prison for that crime of sending another man to kill Lew Bender. Perhaps, after all, there was a sufficient justice done without going so far. All that could be adduced against Blackie was the merest hearsay. There was the testimony of the

274

Mexican, to be sure. And that might have been enough in itself, except that it was proved by Blackie's lawyer, that José Ridal had been raving as he died. So the jury disagreed, and Blackie was set free.

There are condemnations, however, which are purely nonlegal and which cut far deeper than a judge's sentence, and this popular verdict was so heavily against Blackie that he found his life could never again be lived in the West.

He turned his face East, and he carried with him the consolation of knowing that Andy Connell would always support—however meagerly—his adopted son. That was enough for Blackie.

And now that one dream of wealth and prosperity was closed to him, he straightway prepared for new schemes. He closed the door upon that section of his life and resolutely forgot it and all that was behind the door.

Never again did he receive a stab of pain from those old days, except through a little newspaper clipping, which told of the betrothal, a year or two later, of Mr Oliver Hardwick and Beatrice Greenough.

Thus the inheritance of Red was complete.